STAR CROSSED

GEMINI NIGHT

BY BONNIE HEARN HILL

RP | TEENS
PHILADELPHIA • LONDON

STAR CROSSED

GEMINI NIGHT

BY BONNIE HEARN HILL

To Karene Conlin & Roxene Lee,
sisters of my heart

What's your sign?
Check out ours.

Jeremy. Hot Taurus and the only guy for me. He's out of the country, though, and I can't seem to get in touch with him. I have to keep reminding myself that Taurus is one of the most loyal signs in the zodiac.

Henry Jaffa. Famous writer and **Aquarius.** Which means he lives in his head (same as I do) and is out to save the world (just like me). This offbeat mentor of mine has tried to land me an internship with *CRUSH*, a new teen mag based in San Francisco. The rest is up to the editor—and the stars.

Stacy. *CRUSH* editor and Jaffa-ite. She thinks astrology is stupid. With her fondness for the spotlight, she could be a **Leo.** But she has offered me the challenge of a lifetime. If I succeed, I'll have the job of my dreams. If I fail . . . I can't even think about that.

Sol. Sensitive **Cancer** editor of our school newspaper. I know he's into me, but my heart belongs to Jeremy.

Kat. Act-first-ask-questions-later **Aries** cheerleader. She hates me even more now that she knows *CRUSH* will be coming to our school for a beach photo shoot. This hothead is determined to be in it, whatever the cost.

Dina. Kat's **Virgo** sidekick. True to her sign, she is a perfectionist. And critical beyond belief. Now that her best friend is determined to star in the photo shoot, the scheming gossip is out to cause trouble for my friends and me.

Paige. My loyal **Pisces** friend, she has taken up the rear for too long. *Dream* is Pisces' middle name, and this one dreams of being a fashion designer. The *CRUSH* launch party on Halloween finally may be her time to stop dreaming and take action.

Graciela Perez. Known as the Platinum Dragon. This glam **Libra** fashion designer shares her sign's love of beauty. Will our killer costumes that Paige designed for the party win her admiration?

Alex Keen. Young celebrity chef, and the latest obsession of my **Gemini** BFF Chili. But he's a **Sagittarius**, known for traveling from place to place and person to person. Chili's decided he's going to be her date for the costume party, and when that Gemini wants something, look out.

Arianna Woods. Pop star and **Gemini** train wreck. Her chart shows nothing but trouble for the night of the launch party. But she is the magazine cover model, and she is going to be there, baggage and all.

Cory Scott. Arianna's one-time boyfriend and bandmate. A **Scorpio** with deep feelings (and hot looks), he's actually nice to me. An interview with him in the school newspaper might show my classmates that I'm not what Dina is claiming I am.

Josh Mellick. Also a former bandmate, and the guy Arianna loves. What caused their breakup? How does he really feel about her? If he's true to his hardworking **Capricorn** sign, his career is going to come first.

And me, **Logan McRae**, amateur astrologer and textbook **Aquarius**. Everywhere I turn, I run into Geminis. Chili. Arianna Woods. And the last week of October, a Leo Moon squaring Scorpio in Mercury, another Fixed sign. A time of lies, secrets, and disaster. Halloween. It is going to be a Gemini night.

THE TAURUS-AQUARIUS RELATIONSHIP IS FULL OF BUMPS AND BRUISES. NOT THAT EITHER OF YOU MOVES ALL THAT FAST. TAURUS IS EARTH, AND AQUARIUS IS AIR. BECAUSE YOU ARE BOTH FIXED SIGNS, YOU ARE EACH CONVINCED YOU ARE RIGHT, WITH A CAPITAL R. WHEN TAURUS PUSHES, AQUARIUS STEPS BACK. IF YOU WANT THIS RELATIONSHIP TO WORK, THE BULL MUST STEP SOFTLY, AND THE WATER BEARER MUST REACH OUT.

—Fearless Astrology

Terra Bella Beach had never seemed so lonely.

If I, Logan McRae, had paid more attention to *Fearless Astrology*, maybe I wouldn't be so miserable right now. Maybe I wouldn't have fallen for a Taurus. Jeremy had pushed. I had stepped back. And then I had stepped forward in a big way, a way that would and did change his life. Even though I was back home, and he was in Ireland, in my mind, I could still see the plane that carried him disappearing like a silver streak into the sky.

That was almost three months ago. In spite of his e-mails from Ireland, I wasn't sure when or if this boy I couldn't stop thinking about would return. "I still love you," he told me each time we spoke. "Everything is the same." Only nothing was.

To make my life even more unsettled, my mother had arrived home from her golf tour the day I returned from my summer workshop. Then she and Dad had sat me down at the kitchen counter, no less, for the *we-love-you-very-much* talk. Translation: divorce.

Mom had assured me that she'd do her best to spend time at home when her schedule permitted. Dad had said that Gram Janie would move in after Christmas. Everything would be the same, they told me. Except nothing would be.

I had been sitting there, on a stool at the kitchen counter, staring at them and trying not to cry, when the phone rang.

"Logan? Hello. It's Henry Jaffa."

As if I hadn't recognized the voice.

"Hi," I squawked.

"Logan," he said. "I have what could be an amazing opportunity for you."

onday morning in Terra Bella Beach. I had put on my black T-shirt with *Writers Camp* stenciled across it in purple. It would be nice to have a chest to go with it. Then I pulled on my yellow hoodie from the summer, remembering how I'd felt when Jeremy had held me.

I rode to school with my two best friends in Chili's Spyder. She and I sat in front. Paige leaned over from the backseat to catch our conversation above the music.

When I told them about the phone call from Jaffa and the possibility of working as an intern for *CRUSH* magazine, they both screamed.

"I knew it," Paige said.

Chili gave me a one-armed hug. "Oh Logan. You may have lost Jeremy, but you have a famous writer as a mentor."

"Thanks." My eyes stung.

"She hasn't lost Jeremy," Paige said in a soft Pisces voice. "Not necessarily."

"Right." Chili, like many born in her Gemini Sun sign, lied about as well as a five-year-old. "I just meant that having a famous author for a mentor is the best."

The music on the radio drilled into my head.

"Can we ditch Arianna Woods?" I asked.

"This song's better than her last." Chili pulled into the Terra High parking lot and shut off the music. Then she drew back, and the look of concern on her face reminded me of Stella, her very hands-on Armenian mom.

"You're not moving to New York or anything, are you?"

"The magazine is published in San Francisco," I said. "I can commute."

They screamed again. Then, we got out of the car. For a moment, we just looked at each other. Chili in her cropped white sweater over a black tank and jeans, the sunlight glinting off her streaked hair. Paige in a shirt she'd designed herself, pale blue, to match her eyes, but something was different. Makeup. Was Paige really wearing makeup?

As we walked to class, Chili asked, "If *CRUSH* is in San Francisco, how will you be able to intern there? That's ninety minutes each way."

"I'm hoping the school, namely Ms. Snider, will go along with the plan. It's only one day a week."

Our hardworking Capricorn journalism teacher had cut me some slack last year when I was a sophomore, and I needed her support again.

We walked out of the parking lot, and as Chili and Paige headed for their first period classes, I started toward the journalism room.

Just then I noticed crazy Kat, the Aries cheerleader as she came around a corner. Her short, black hair was pushed back behind her ears. When she noticed me, she grinned.

"Hey, Logan. Did you hear about Nathan and Geneva?"

"No." I kept walking.

She ran up along side me. "They're going to Maui in November."

"Good for them." I didn't turn to look at her, just kept on heading toward the journalism class.

"They'll be traveling with Nathan's family. His parents

love Geneva."

Finally, I met her eyes. "And you're telling me this, because?"

She gave me a superior smirk. "Because I thought you'd want to know."

"What they do doesn't concern me, Kat," I said. "They're in college. I'm here. Besides, I have a new boyfriend."

"Oh, really? Who?"

"His name is Jeremy." Best not to mention that he was in Ireland, and that I had no idea when I would see him again.

"Oh." I could tell that I'd taken her by surprise and that she was trying to come up with a fiery Aries insult. "How'd you manage that? Did you use astrology on him?"

As if it were a magic trick that would snag me any guy I wanted.

"In a way." That should give her something to gossip about. I didn't care.

Ms. Snider stepped out of the classroom. Ever the perfect Capricorn in her crisp little brown tunic and cream-colored turtleneck, she looked hot. The rumor was that she was dating my English teacher, Mr. Franklin, but they hadn't gone public with it.

"Good morning," she said.

"Hi, Ms. Snider. Um, could I talk to you for a minute?"

"About Henry Jaffa?" Her expression got a little less friendly. "You know I'm proud of you, Logan, but you shouldn't have asked Jaffa to pressure me."

"What are you talking about? I didn't ask him to do anything."

"Really? Then why did he contact me last night?"

"I swear I don't know."

"Well, he called the superintendent." Color rose along her cheeks. "As you can imagine, I don't appreciate such manipulation from anyone, not even a well-known writer."

"Henry Jaffa is not a manipulator," I said before I remembered that I was talking back to a teacher. "He's very straightforward, and he's not the type to pull strings."

"Well, he's certainly pulling them, or trying to."

Kat stared openly, no doubt taking mental notes for Geneva.

"Could we go inside?" I asked Snider. "I'd like to talk to you without an audience."

"Don't flatter yourself." Kat said under her breath, but she didn't move.

Snider seemed to take it in. "All right. Shall we walk down the hall?"

Good idea. Students would be filling the journalism room any minute.

"I didn't know that Mr. Jaffa contacted you," I told her. "All I said to him is that I would need the approval of the school. Maybe that's why he phoned the superintendent, and since you're my journalism teacher . . ."

"Whatever the reason, I got called, at home, on a Sunday and hit with considerable pressure from a famous writer."

"I am sorry if I caused any of that," I said. "I was just so excited about the internship. If you can help me get it, I'll make up the time."

"Are you still involved with that astrology stuff?"

Yes, Capricorn, and don't be so true-to-your-sign frosty about it. "I am," I said. "It's what I used last spring when everything here was in such an uproar." *Not to mention your reputation.* I didn't say it, but I could tell by her expression that she understood.

"What happened last spring was all about your courage and your intelligence," she said. "And, yes, I know how much you want to believe otherwise."

"But what does that have to do with my internship?" I asked.

"Only this." She lowered her voice. "Henry Jaffa."

"What about him?"

"His beliefs, the subjects he writes about. All of that paranormal stuff." She paused in the hall. "You're a good kid, Logan. I want you to learn to rely on yourself and not on magic."

"Astrology isn't magic," I said. "And *CRUSH* is a teen magazine. I know the superintendent will go along with the internship if you approve."

"Okay," she said. "I will do that on two conditions."

"Anything," I managed to say.

"First, you can go to the magazine only one day a week."

"No problem. That's the way the internship is set up."

"Second, you have to promise me that you'll stay away from astrology."

"Totally away?"

"Away," she said. "Promise me that you will not use it to run your life."

That was easy. Astrology didn't run my life. It enhanced and expanded my life.

"It's a deal," I told her.

NOTES TO SELF

It's happened. It's going to take a lot of extra work, and I'll have a lot of make-up assignments, but I now have approval to intern at the magazine every Friday, starting four days from tonight. The moon will be in Gemini, meaning that my Air sign communication skills should be at their best. So, yes, I am thinking about astrology again right now, but not in a magical way. In a hopeful way.

MOON CYCLES

Every thirty days, the moon changes from new to full, from the invisible black moon, to the round, yellow moon. As it travels, it changes signs every two-and-a-half days. The moon's changes will affect you, based on your sign, your element, and other factors you will soon understand.

Aries Moon *Look for action and impulsiveness. Know that tempers can flare, yours included.*

Taurus Moon *You may feel more laid-back. And even the meekest signs may be more stubborn.*

Gemini Moon *You may find yourself running off at the mouth about a variety of subjects. Be careful about taking on too many projects or assignments.*

Cancer Moon *This is the time to adopt a puppy or take a cooking class. Your actions will be best served if they revolve around your home.*

Leo Moon *An absolutely social moon. This is a great time for even the most timid signs to go out and make new friends.*

Virgo Moon *With this moon, you can get organized and go shopping for bargains. It's also an excellent time to balance your checkbook and make a budget.*

Libra Moon *This is the romantic moon, the moon of beauty. Fall in love, get in touch with an old love, or indulge your self-love at a spa.*

Scorpio Moon *Great passion. Push yourself to do something. Finish that assignment. Write that report.*

Sagittarius Moon *This is the adventure moon. Go on a road trip with no map. Have fun. Don't commit to anything but your sense of play and your wonderful optimism.*

Capricorn Moon *When you need to sit down for some clear-headed thinking, this is the moon that can influence such efforts. Because of Capricorn's inherent elegance, it's also an ideal time to shop for a sophisticated look.*

Aquarius Moon *This is the time to look at the pros and cons of working out a problem. It's also a friendship moon. Consider volunteering or joining a club.*

Pisces Moon *This is the time to trust your instincts. Intuitive Pisces is also a creative moon. Write that poem. Pick up that paintbrush. Dream that dream.*

2

Although Aquarius is usually focused on a goal, it's also important to focus on those around you who have the power to help you meet that goal. Or not. A Fire sign would crash through the door, and an Earth sign would dig its heels in. A Water sign would reduce everything to emotion, be hurt, and say nothing. If you're an Air sign, your mind is like a complicated machine trying to get from here to there. Stop thinking and start talking. You know you want to.

—*Fearless Astrology*

earless Astrology was right again. I needed to stop speculating and start talking. Having Jaffa for my mentor was a huge plus, but he wouldn't be able to control my internship at the magazine. Stacy Rogers would. Although she had seemed a little cool during our telephone interview, she had given me the job. Now, I just needed to prove to her that I was worthy of it. I would do that, not by crashing my way through the door the way a Fire sign would, but by talking my way through it like a Gemini or the Aquarius that I am.

The *CRUSH* offices were on the second floor of a building on Powell and Union Street in North Beach. The months of September, October, even November were San Francisco's real summer. The day was warm enough for short sleeves, but experience had taught me to dress in layers. Even though fall was my favorite time to visit the city, I knew that the weather could do an about-face in an instant. At any moment, the fog could roll in and change everything.

The boots I wore were a gift from Paige, who had insisted they would make me look taller—and, yes, maybe a little older. The vehicle I had driven here was my dad's ugly Chevy paint van he used to deliver his artwork to galleries and page proofs to his advertising clients. I parked it in a garage about a half-block away where no one could possibly see me. Then I started walking down Powell.

Between two large, bushy trees, I spotted the burgundy-and-gold awning of Washington Square Bar and Grill. Those bay windows, trimmed in white, against a yellow back-ground, looked as if they belonged in a Victorian home. The building where *CRUSH* was located must be straight ahead.

"Logan. Over here."

Thank goodness. There was Jaffa wrapped in the same navy scarf he'd lived in during our summer workshop. I was so happy to see him, his frizzy hair even wilder in the warm breeze, I could have hugged him.

Except that Jaffa wasn't a hugger. He was a focused, kind-of-weird Aquarius. He grinned just then as if he were a mad scientist, and I a bug under his microscope.

"I told you we'd get approval from your school, didn't I?"

"You did. I'm so happy." I didn't mention that my Capricorn journalism teacher wasn't.

"You'll like Stacy," he said. "She's very ambitious and ded-icated, the same as you. If you get along as well as I think you're going to, perhaps you might try for something more than an internship."

"Something more?" I asked.

"An astrology column, for instance." He gave me a pleased-with-himself grin and stopped to examine some flowers from a sidewalk vendor. "I need to send something to my wife."

I was still thinking about the astrology column and remembering my no-astrology promise to Snider.

"I don't think you can ship those," I told him. "What's your wife's Sun sign?"

"Aries." He continued to eye the flowers. *Good combination.*

The Fire sign wife was running the relationship while he was trying to save the world.

"Maybe you should just call her," I said. "She'd probably like to know that you're thinking about her. Aries women often want to be the center of their loved one's life."

"Great idea. Actually, she gets upset when I don't call often enough. Thanks for reminding me." He turned away from the flowers. "You are going to be a fine astrology writer, and this is where we're going to try to make it happen."

My mind exploded with reasons why I couldn't go after more than I already had. Snider would be angry and end my internship. That was at the top of the list. Right along with how I could possibly write an astrology column for a national magazine.

"Don't you think I should prove myself as an intern before I ask for a column?"

Jaffa stopped before a building of weathered bricks. "Remember this, Logan. Everything in life is action or distraction."

"Action or distraction?"

"If it's not moving you forward, it's distraction, regardless of how noble or how interesting it appears at the time."

"But what if *CRUSH* already has an astrology columnist?"

"Do you know where I would be if I had worried about *what if*?" He gave me that same weird grin I remembered from class when he was trying to drive a point home.

"Sure," I said. "But you're Henry Jaffa."

"I wasn't always."

Good point. I started to say that I appreciated his confidence in me, but just then an elegant girl in a sapphire-blue jacket stepped out of a taxi at the curb in front of us.

"Henry." She ran to us and took both of Jaffa's hands in hers.

Her thick black hair was pulled straight back, no bangs, just those dark eyes that dominated her face. I tried to guess her age. Late twenties. Jaffa must be right about her ambition and dedication. Her skin was pale as porcelain, her lip gloss muted and natural. With that hair, she had to be a Leo, I thought. She wanted to be on stage, and right now, with Jaffa beaming at her, she was.

"Hey, Stacy." He turned to me. "This is Logan."

"Welcome." She put out her hand with the understated-but-perfect nails that matched her lips.

"It's so good to meet you in person," I said.

"You, too. Sorry I'm late. I just got back from an appointment with Arianna Woods and her people. She's going to be our first cover model for *CRUSH*, but of course you know that."

"Arianna Woods?" No, I hadn't known that, and, apparently, neither had Jaffa.

"Isn't she having some issues?" he asked.

"Just a little negative press. She's okay now, better than okay, and she will be a great cover for our debut issue. Don't you think so, Logan?"

"I'm sure she will," I said.

"I mean, you're our target demographic. Wouldn't you want to read a magazine with Arianna on the cover?"

I tried really hard. "I wouldn't *not* want to read it." *Lousy, lousy Aquarius liar.*

"Well, then. Is there someone you'd rather see on the cover? Someone who'd make you pick it up or subscribe to it?"

I was starting to feel sweaty and anxious. I knew she wanted me to say no, but I couldn't. "Girls like guys. So, I don't know. Maybe Josh Mellick. He and Cory Scott have done pretty well even after Arianna left their group. And Josh was on the cover of *People* a few months ago."

"Magazines like ours have *girls* on the covers," she said. "We'll have guys inside, of course. Maybe even Josh or Cory. I really do think Arianna's perfect, in spite of her . . . alleged problems."

"If anyone can make it work," Jaffa said, "I am certain you can. Now, I need to get back to my hotel."

"I was hoping we could all have lunch." I could tell that Stacy was disappointed to be stuck with me.

He shook his head in that unaware, onto-his-next-mission Aquarius way. "I'm on deadline, same as you."

I was reminded that this was *the* Henry Jaffa and that I was beyond lucky to even know him, not to mention have him on my side.

"Thanks so much for making this happen," I told him, "and for taking the time to meet me here."

"You two will work well together," he said. "My instincts regarding these matters are seldom wrong."

Stacy smiled at him, and I could see that even though she was a magazine editor now, she was just as in awe as I was.

Jaffa-ites. That's what the writers he mentored called themselves. I hoped to be one of them someday.

"Henry says you're a hard worker," she told me. "The intern we tried before you was all about the glamour. I don't have to explain to you about unrealistic expectations."

"No, you don't. I'll do any job you want me to." I realized that Jaffa was staring at me. "I'm also . . . I mean, I am kind of into astrology. I'm just putting it out there in case you ever have a need for something like that."

Although she looked as friendly as ever, I could feel the air freeze between us.

"Henry told me about what happened in Monterey this summer. It's a little difficult to believe that astrology had much to do with it."

"If you were there," Jaffa said, "you wouldn't question."

He was trying to help me. So I couldn't just stand there, too terrified to speak.

"It was a forty-year-old mystery that no one had been able to solve until then," I told her in a voice that sounded far more confident than I felt. "It wouldn't have happened if I hadn't studied the astrological charts of the people involved."

"That may or may not be, but I think these magazine astrology columns are clichés. And, yes, we are looking for one, but I'm going to have to find a real astrologer or at least a reasonable astrology service. As much as I like your sincere approach, Logan, you're still only a high school student."

"The same as your readers. Why wouldn't teens want to

read an astrology column by a teen?" I asked.

"She's right," Jaffa said. "It's one way you can get past the cliché, Stacy. A *teen* astrology writer."

"I don't know." She looked from him to me, as if trying to decide how much denying my request would harm her relationship with him. Finally, she said, "Okay, so here's what's happening. We're going to do a Halloween launch party for the magazine, a costume party."

"That sounds wonderful." I wasn't sure what she wanted from me. "Are you saying that I might be able to attend?"

"Of course, but more than that, I am going to give you the birth date of one of the celebs we've invited to be there. You then have to do the person's chart and predict their future."

"How much of their future?" I asked, and wondered what I'd gotten myself into.

"Just the month ahead," she told me. "The same way you would do in the magazine. Deadline will be the day of the party. If your predictions come close enough, I'll consider you for a contract as our teen astrologer."

"Consider?" I asked.

Henry chuckled, and Stacy laughed too.

"Okay, Logan. Here's the deal. Figure out this one chart correctly for me, and you have the job for six months at least. We'll give you a contract."

"I can do it," I said. "No problem."

Yeah, right.

NOTES TO SELF

Thank you, Jaffa. Thank you very much. You've given Stacy enough confidence in me that she is actually considering me as a columnist. Even though she doesn't believe in astrology. Even though she thinks I am too young despite these boots that Paige said made me look sophisticated. So now all I have to do is figure out this chart. Double Gemini with an Aries Moon. That's a no-brainer. Arianna Woods. Everything she does is Gemini. Now, what do I say to Ms. Snider next week in class? That's pretty easy for this Aquarius.

Nothing.

3

NOTHING ABOUT THE ZODIAC IS CLEAR-CUT. THE CAR-
DINAL SIGNS ARE THOUGHT OF AS LEADERS, FOR
INSTANCE, YET SOMETIMES THEY ARE SIDETRACKED BY
A NEED FOR ATTENTION. ALTHOUGH FIXED SIGNS CAN
BE STABLE, THEY CAN FREQUENTLY GET STUCK BY
REFUSING TO LET GO OF THE SAME-OLD SAME-OLD.
MUTABLE SIGNS POSSESS FLEXIBILITY, BUT TOO MUCH
FLEXIBILITY CAN LEAVE YOU TIED IN KNOTS. REMEM-
BER THAT EACH SIGN HAS A POSITIVE AND A NEGATIVE
SIDE. BEING AWARE OF BOTH WILL BETTER PREPARE
YOU FOR SUCCESS.

—Fearless Astrology

CARDINAL, FIXED, MUTABLE: WHICH ARE YOU?

CARDINAL: *Aries, Libra, Cancer, Capricorn*
FIXED: *Taurus, Leo, Scorpio, Aquarius*
MUTABLE: *Gemini, Virgo, Sagittarius, Pisces*

already knew I was a Fixed sign, and, yes, I was well aware that I had to get unstuck in order to have a chance at a column with *CRUSH*. Even the thought of it sent terror through me. And hope.

At least I really did know something about astrology now. When I first found the book, I was clueless about how to figure out a chart. Now I knew that with only the birth date, I could find out everything except a person's Rising sign. Fortunately, Stacy had given me that too. Arianna was a double Gemini, with both her Sun and Rising in that sign of communication. Her Moon was in Aries, the Ram, as was her Mars. No wonder she went after what she wanted with little regard for anyone else. Her Venus was in Pisces, the sign of the dreamer who believed in Prince Charming and the fairy-tale ending. That was a surprise.

One thing I did well was focus on a task, so that's what I forced myself to do, starting with some online research on Arianna. I didn't have to go past her YUTalk page. Right there, it proclaimed:

Arianna Woods
Motto: *Don't even try it.*
Hair: *Fake*
Eyes: *Hazel*
Sun Sign: *Gemini*
Music: *Everything*
Goal: *Race the Death Machine all the way to hell*

Now, that was an uplifting thought. It was followed by some pretty hot stuff pertaining to guys. A Mutable sign for sure, with some Cardinal Aries thrown in there. Would it help me or hurt me to suggest that Stacy try to get her to change the bio before Arianna showed up as the face of *CRUSH*'s first issue?

But at least I had figured out the mystery chart on my first try. Arianna was a Gemini, and probably a pretty messed-up one. Although she was only a couple of years older than I, the information on her site failed to hide how disturbed she looked beneath the makeup and the multicolored hair extensions. What was that race the death machine stuff all about? Was it part of the act, or did she mean it? And it was up to me to predict what would happen to her in the month ahead. I would attempt that as soon as I checked out the ephemeris and found out a little more.

EPHEMERIS

*A Latin word that comes from the Greek "ephémeros, -on,"
meaning daily. An almanac listing the positions of the planets
and other data for any given time period covering six thousand
years. A tool used by astrologers in forecasting. As with any
tool, its effectiveness is based, in part, upon the skill of the user.*

I sent Jeremy a text late Friday night after I had driven home.

```
call when u can
I need to talk
And I love u
```

Since he was a musician, he might know something about
Arianna. Besides, he'd be happy that I'd found such an *amazing opportunity*, as Jaffa put it.

Right. I couldn't lie about it to myself. It wasn't Arianna
or the internship. It wasn't even the possibility of a column.
It was loneliness. I needed to hear Jeremy's voice, needed to
hear him say he loved me.

By Monday, he still hadn't called. Nor had he replied to my
text. That was a first.

I tried to drive the doubts from my mind by singing louder
than I could think in the shower. Channeled Beyoncé. Channeled Gwen Stefani. Even channeled Arianna Woods. *"Love
me just a little bit, a little bit, a little . . ."* I showered in words,
swam in them.

The steam didn't do much for my out-of-control curls. My hair looked as if it belonged in a cartoon.

How could a guy like Jeremy fall for someone with a flat chest, a nonexistent butt, and hair like mine? It wasn't the thought I wanted to think as I stared into the bathroom mirror. I closed my eyes and pictured the beach in Monterey, the two of us that last day at the airport.

Everything in life is action or distraction.

I could hear Henry Jaffa, could see that strange little smile. Beating myself up in the mirror was most definitely distraction. And so was daydreaming about Jeremy. I needed to focus today.

That meant wearing the new tank and jacket my mom bought the weekend of the GDA (Great Divorce Announcement). And the boots again. Yes, definitely the boots. I pulled my hair up in back with a little braid on the side, and I was ready to go.

When they picked me up for school that Monday morning, Chili and Paige said I looked hot. I realized it was the first time in a long time I had heard that from them. Maybe that's because it was the first time in a long time that I had cared about how I looked at school. I really hoped that Jeremy would show up and take me away at any moment. Now that he wasn't answering my text, I could somehow see myself more clearly again. And I wanted to like what I saw. Today—my first Monday back from San Francisco—I did. Kind of, and for an Aquarius, kind of was just fine.

In journalism class, Snider asked us to work in groups of three to brainstorm story ideas. I started for a table but noticed that Chili was walking slower than usual. Sol, our editor, caught up with us.

"Like your hair," he whispered.

Not what I wanted to hear. Not from him. He was a tall, soft-spoken Cancer who had moved with his family from Texas at the end of my sophomore year. Although I liked him, he was coming on a little too strong, especially for such an easygoing guy.

"Thanks."

I glanced away from him and slid onto a chair.

"Mind if I join you?" He looked around at us as if not certain how to proceed.

"You're the editor." I didn't mean to make it sound harsh, but it came out that way. "I mean sure," I said.

"Have a seat," Chili told him, in that hyperfake way she used when she was up to something.

I wasn't certain what was going on, but I didn't like it. I especially didn't like Sol pulling up a chair next to me and crowding my personal space.

"We need to come up with a great feature story. Any ideas?" He gazed at me with that kind of cute lopsided smile, and I felt even more uncomfortable.

"People," I said. "Kids always like reading about other kids."

"We've got to do better than that."

Chili and I exchanged glances.

"Sol, are you worried?" Chili asked. "Is it because the newspaper won all of those awards when Geneva was editor? Is the pressure on for you to come up with something extra outstanding?"

Go for it, Air sign. Speak first, think later.

"Well, sure, that's part of it. But I'd also like to produce a newspaper that isn't cookie-cutter high school, you know? Too bad we couldn't have kept your astrology column, Logan." He gave me that look again.

"Snider made it pretty clear that she doesn't want to reinstate it."

"I know that, but maybe we can come up with another column for you. After working with Henry Jaffa, you deserve it."

I didn't want Sol's column, and I definitely didn't want to owe him any favors. "I'm going to be pretty busy with *CRUSH*," I said.

"She might get a column there," Chili said.

"What kind of column?"

I shot her a look, but all I got in return was that Gemini little-kid shrug.

"Well, I'm not really sure exactly."

"That's it." Chili said. "That's what she needs to write about, Sol, her internship, all of the famous people she's going to meet at the magazine, all the parties." She flashed him a confident smile. "She's good friends with Henry Jaffa. He calls her at home. And she even knows Arianna Woods, kind of."

"You know Arianna?" Sol asked.

"No, I don't. I've studied her sign a little. That's all Chili meant. She is going to be on the first *CRUSH* cover."

"What sign is she? And is she really as clueless as she pretends to be?" Great. Now he thought I was the gossip queen of Terra Bella Beach.

"I have no idea." As much as I needed to diffuse this conversation, I still wanted him to know that I wasn't some phony. "She is a Gemini, a Mutable Air sign. Flexible communicator, okay?"

"What's her Moon?" Chili chimed in. True to the information-junkie aspect of her sign, she would soon be discussing Arianna's Mars and Venus.

"Aries."

"What does that mean?" he asked. "My dad's an Aries. What are you?"

No mistaking it. Sol was into me. And he was cute and nice. But he was not Jeremy, not even close. I ignored the question.

"An Aries Sun like your dad's is different from an Aries Moon," I told him. "And Arianna already has a Gemini Sun. Either way, it means fire and drive. The combination could make her even more out there than she already is."

"What do you think is going to happen to her?" he asked. "Is she totally over?"

"I might be able to figure it out with the ephemeris." Okay, I was showing off a little but I couldn't help myself. "That's what I'm going to do in order to get the column with *CRUSH*, try to figure out what issues she might have."

"The ephemeris is a way of forecasting," Chili told Sol before he could ask. "Logan can access it on her computer." She grinned at me as if to say: *Please just like this guy, will you?*

I shook my head. "I said I was going to *try* to figure it out. I didn't say I could do it."

"Can you forecast anything for Cancer?" he asked.

"Maybe." I reached for my phone, took it out, and hid it inside my binder.

A few taps on the keypad and I was online. A few more, and the ephemeris came up. Chili scrambled into the chair beside me. I held the phone lower and motioned to Sol. "Check it out."

He slid his seat even closer to me. "What do all of those numbers and symbols mean?"

"The symbols at the top are called glyphs. Look, that's Sun, Moon, Mercury, Venus, Mars. The days are listed on the side."

Chili beamed at him. "Didn't I tell you she was smart?"

So that was it. Chili had said something to get Sol interested in me. How humiliating.

He nodded and moved closer to me. I pushed back my chair.

"What are you doing over here?" Snider's voice was Capricorn cold. How long had she been watching us?

"We're just discussing story ideas." I pulled the phone closer to me.

"I warned you, Logan," she said, looking at my phone. "How could you bring this stuff into my classroom?"

"I was just explaining something to Sol and Chili," I said. "I didn't mean to bring anything in here."

"She's going to work with Arianna Woods," Sol said. "We were just trying to find out what was going to happen next with her."

"On that?" Snider glared at my phone.

"Yes," I said, unable to lie about the obvious. "I'm . . ."

"Turn it off."

"That's what I'm doing." I reached to press the screen into darkness, and then I got a good look at the ephemeris. The prediction for Arianna Woods. The Aries Moon was squaring Scorpio.

"Why is this taking so long?" Snider demanded. "What are you looking at, Logan?"

"Nothing," I said. But still I tried to make sense of what I was seeing. The Aries Moon would square Scorpio in Mercury, another Fixed sign, for two-and-one-half days at the end of October. I tried to remember what I had read in *Fearless* about Fixed squares. *Secrets. Intense conflict. Frequently spells disaster.*

"What is it?" Snider asked.

"Nothing," I said. "I'm sorry." My voice was trembling, because if what I saw was correct, Arianna Woods might actually be in danger.

NOTES TO SELF

So, this Aquarius is trying to save the world again, but I can't help it. I'm a Fixed sign too, which makes me even more determined to find out the truth. Besides, maybe saving Arianna will keep me from obsessing about Jeremy.

Snider made me stay after class and reminded me—as if I need a reminder—that she could make my internship disappear as easily as she made it happen. Sol, of course, had tried to take the blame, which only made me feel worse. When I confronted Chili later, she denied trying to set me up with him, her lie as blatant as her grin.

A Snider assignment tonight, make that a punishment. I'm supposed to write a first-person account of how it feels to be back here after Monterey. It's not even for the paper, just one of those finding-your-voice exercises she likes so much. "Define home," she said. I'll try to give her what she wants. But here's what I really have to do. Find out everything I can about Arianna Woods, and not just to get the column now. I need to try to stop whatever "intense conflict," maybe even disaster, that is heading her way. And I have to do it fast.

BEACH TOWN

By Logan McRae

Terra Bella Beach is like any other small town, except that it backs up next to the ocean. Somehow its lack of sophistication makes it cooler, more relaxed. Younger. Not that there aren't a lot of older people here, because there are, but they are different old. Take Manny, the retired dairy farmer, who runs the ice cream shop on the pier. Or Joyce, the seventy-something lady who wears glitter in her dyed red hair. She says she was once on Broadway. Now, as she walks along the beach with her cane, she serenades anyone within hearing distance with her rendition of "Hello, Dolly!" and "What a Wonderful World." Going to school here means learning the language of the beach. Our favorite words are "hella" and "dude," and we use them so often that I bet we'll wear them out before another year passes. The language is part of being in the beach town club, though. It keeps us connected, most of the time, at least. Here's a quick guide.

• **Freakin'** *"That's freakin' disgusting."*

• **Ridiculous** *"That's absolutely ridiculous." Or ri-dic, if the goal is to convey even more sarcasm.*

• **Hella** *"He's hella hot!" Hella's an adjective that makes any noun or adjective sound better.*

• **Like** *"It's like, something we do all the time." My dad says they used this word in his day, so maybe it's one of those terms like "cool," that like never gets old.*

• **Dude** *"Dude, what the hell is going on!?"*

So much for the language. Except for some personal issues, I'm glad to be back here. The place has a rhythm to it, a sound that is partially the tide crashing in and rolling out, and partially the cries of the gulls. It looks, smells, and sounds like home. I am glad it's my home.

How dishonest is this? But at least I didn't mention anything about astrology.

4

IN YOUR EFFORTS TO IMPRESS OR ACHIEVE, REMEMBER THAT SOME SIGNS ARE NATURAL SHOW-STEALERS. THE FIRE SIGNS OF ARIES, LEO, AND SAGITTARIUS BREAK THROUGH ANY DOOR, EACH IN A DIFFERENT WAY. EARTH SIGNS, TAURUS, VIRGO, AND CAPRICORN, GET THERE IN SURE, MEASURED STEPS. GEMINI, LIBRA, AND AQUARIUS, THE AIR SIGNS, TALK THEIR WAY TO SUCCESS. EMOTIONAL CANCER, SCORPIO, AND PISCES, THE WATER SIGNS, ARE SOMETIMES OVERSHADOWED BY MORE ASSERTIVE COMPETITION. THEY WILL REACH THEIR GOALS ONCE THEY REALIZE THAT THEY MUST GO AFTER THE PRIZE AND NOT WAIT FOR THE PRIZE TO COME TO THEM.

—Fearless Astrology

*W*ell, I had certainly tried to talk my way out of Snider's wrath, but I had been too disturbed by what the ephemeris appeared to be revealing. For the rest of the week, I researched Arianna Woods in every spare moment—early days with the band *Mellick*, leaving the group, trashy photos of her that had shown up on the Internet, the cancellation of a film role, and her new release—the same song that Chili played nonstop in her car.

It didn't take high-tech research to find out that Arianna had briefly dated Cory Scott, and after him, Josh Mellick, the bass man in their band back then. The tabloids had kept track. She had left both guys to pursue the solo career that had at first peaked, and then delivered her to the cover of *CRUSH* for what, I realized, might be her last chance. How did one earn a last chance at age twenty-one?

On Friday, I returned to San Francisco. As Stacy had told me, the job wasn't glamorous, but after the summer workshop with Jaffa, I already knew how to work. I made phone calls, faxed and e-mailed press releases, and even did a coffee run for the editorial meeting that afternoon.

Stacy looked up from her desk and surveyed the assortment of coffees I presented to her. Today she was dressed entirely in peach with her dark hair still pulled straight back. Her nails matched her lips. Her lips matched the scarf wrapped around her pale shoulders. She had a mean beauty. Not that she was a mean person. I hadn't figured that out yet. She was just one of those rare women who was even more attractive when she wasn't smiling. Maybe that's why she did so little of it.

If the room were a stage in a theater, she would have been in the center of it, lit by the spotlight. The girl must be a Leo or maybe an Aries. There had to be Fire in her sign.

"I wanted mine without whip," she said.

"The art director's is the one with whip." I handed her the other cup. "This is yours."

"Thanks." She stood to let me know it was time for me to leave.

"Would it be all right if I stayed for the staff meeting?" I asked. "Since I'm here anyway."

"Sure, if you want to." I could almost see her thinking what Henry Jaffa would say if she denied me. "Yes, of course. I should have suggested it. It's just that . . ."

"What?" I asked.

"I was a little disappointed about your reaction to Arianna Woods as our first cover model."

"I shouldn't have said anything."

"Actually, you didn't say anything, but you made it clear what you thought."

"I like her music," I kind-of lied. "I really do."

"Then why wouldn't you be thrilled that she's going to be on our cover?"

"Have you ever checked out her blog on the YUTalk?" I asked. "All that ride-the-death-train stuff? And the guys?"

"What are you talking about?"

"See for yourself." I felt like a total jerk. Here I was treating Arianna like an enemy, and I didn't even know her.

Stacy began clicking on her keyboard. "Why didn't anyone

tell me about this?"

"Maybe it's okay, but it just seemed . . ."

"It certainly isn't okay. We have to change it right now." She picked up her phone. "Danielle, did you check out Arianna's presence on the Internet? You did? Then why the hell didn't you tell me about her YUTalk page? What? Well, why don't you go take a look, and then we can discuss it. I've got an e-mail to write."

She hung up, without saying good-bye, then hammered on her keyboard. I could only imagine what message Arianna's team was going to receive, and how she would react.

"Thanks for alerting me to this." Stacy gave me a straight-lipped smile. "I'm sorry I misjudged your attitude, and I think Henry was right about our working well together, after all."

I loved the *working well together* part but wasn't too excited about the *after all*.

"I'd like that," I said.

"And of course you can stay for the meeting. Our spring issue of *CRUSH* will feature *Beaches We Love*. I know you're from a beach town, so feel free to chime in."

What a difference, and just because I had told her what any of her staff members could have. Which made me wonder why they hadn't. Wasn't such a simple task something her assistant could handle? How difficult was it to do a Web search on the cover celebrity, especially one as troubled as this one was supposed to be?

The others entered the room and picked up their coffee cups. It wasn't a huge meeting, just Mary Elizabeth and

Bobby, the fashion and art directors, Stacy's assistant Danielle, a good-looking guy in charge of sales, and a couple of associate editors.

Mary Elizabeth dressed like a grown-up version of Paige. Today her blond bob was completely hidden by a bright orange paisley scarf. With that mane, she had to be a Leo, or maybe a fiery Aries or Sadge.

Bobby, the overweight art director, was wearing a Hawaiian print shirt. In spite of his thick glasses, he had soulful blue eyes, magnified by the lenses, of course. Earth sign was my first guess, and then I thought of Jeremy. Where was my Taurus, and why hadn't he answered my text?

We all gathered around Stacy's office. Through the bay window, I could see a thin tangle of cable car wires and the gray-and-glass wash of the building across the street.

Bobby balanced his coffee on his Hawaiian-print stomach and settled back in the chair.

"How many beaches will we be covering?" He seemed eager to disagree with the answer, even before he heard it. I wondered if it was because Stacy was so young. In fact, except for Danielle and me, she was the youngest person in the room.

"Eight, maybe ten. We'll use lots of graphics and bullet points about what makes each one different. Maybe some teen stars modeling the suits."

"Everyone does that," he said, and the coffee cup sloshed in his hand. "We need something to make it stand out as more than just another glorified swimsuit ad. My people can do only so much. We need content."

"Why not use real teens as models?" My voice sounded high-pitched and uncertain. Everyone turned to stare at me. I reminded myself that Stacy had told me that I could chime in.

"Too difficult to coordinate," the art guy said.

"I'm not so sure about that," Mary Elizabeth replied. "It's fresh, and our readers might go for it, especially if we say we're making it an annual feature."

"We could pose one girl from each school with a male celebrity," Stacy piped up. "Hot guys, real teen girls. What else do we need?"

As if it was her idea. She glanced at me again as if expecting me to verify that.

"Large and small schools," I said. "Terra Bella Beach would be a great place."

Danielle, Stacy's assistant, glared back at me through her dark-rimmed glasses. She was constantly working, and this was the longest time since I'd arrived that I had seen her sit still. "I don't think so," she said. "We need something with more style and class."

My Gram Janie had told me more than once that people who used the word, "class," sorely lacked it.

"Malibu, Laguna, and San Diego have been done hundreds of times," I said. "Terra Beach isn't what the tourists see, but it's the essence of what living on the California coast is really like. At least take a look at it."

"You are so right." Stacy actually smiled at me, a real smile this time with teeth and everything. "As I've been saying all along, no one thinks of those cute little towns when they think of California. Let's use Terra Bella Beach as one of our locations."

For the first time since she had chosen me for this internship, I believed she might be starting to see me as more than Henry Jaffa's pet.

"It might work." Bobby absently wiped at a coffee stain on his shirt. "We could have some fun with it."

"Little-known beaches." Danielle tossed back her blond hair. "It has great potential, Stace. It really does."

So the world of publishing wasn't all that different from the world of high school, I realized. Everyone debated, and then, when the person on top expressed an opinion, the rest of the crew pretended that they had felt that way all along.

As everyone at the meeting continued to congratulate Stacy for coming up with my idea, I crept out of the room. If anyone asked, I would just say I had taken an early lunch. At the elevator, I took a deep breath. *Just get a grip,* as my Gram would say. So Stacy had stolen my idea. No big deal. If she liked it enough to claim it as her own, maybe she would like me enough to give me the columnist job.

The doors opened, and a blond train wreck stepped out. Her black sparkly top ended at her midriff. The white low-cut jeans were trying hard to show off her assets, but they couldn't make up for the feeling of weary apathy that seemed as much a part of her as the trademark navy-blue eyes. Those eyes stared right through me, that unblinking paparazzi hate expression I'd seen in so many shots of her.

Arianna Woods.

"Hi, Arianna," I said. "I'm Logan, and I'll be . . ."

"Dude. I know who you are," she replied in a voice too old and too harsh for her age. "Thanks for screwing up my day."

NOTES TO SELF

That was my introduction to the girl I had hoped to save from whatever disaster lay in her path. So much for my early lunch, which I didn't want anyway. I followed her back inside, only to have her slam Stacy's door in my face. After a brief meeting, Arianna stalked through the office. She paused briefly before leaving and shot me one final look of pure hate.

At lunch, I summoned the courage to tell Stacy what had happened, and she admitted that she had mentioned that I was the one who had alerted her to the "inconsistencies" of Arianna on YUTalk. Stacy again told me how grateful she was that I had done so. Besides, I didn't have to work directly with Arianna, she said.

Now I'm home, and I am going to check YUTalk again. Arianna's profile looks absolutely virginal.

Nickname: *Ari*
Hair: *Natural blond*
Eyes: *Navy blue*
Sun Sign: *Gemini*
Music: *Everything*
Goal: *Help my fans get in touch with them-
selves through my music.*

The photo of her shows what looks like a religious symbol around her neck. It appears to be made of diamonds.

Is it possible that I am the reason she changed the
page? Afraid so. And if I'm right, that Gemini won't
rest until she gets even. So, we are in a race now. Can
she discredit me before I can save her from whatever
is going to happen on that night of the launch party?
How can I save spacey Arianna from that Gemini night
when I have no idea what is going to go wrong?

SQUARED PLANETS: A HARD ENERGY

*When two planets are ninety degrees apart, it is said that
they square each other. Because of the ninety-degree angle,
squares are approximately three signs apart. Thus a square is
usually Cardinal (Aries, Libra, Cancer, Capricorn), Fixed
(Taurus, Leo, Scorpio, Aquarius), or Mutable (Gemini, Virgo,*

Sagittarius, Pisces) and will take on the qualities of each. A Cardinal square will involve power struggles. A Fixed square will be unyielding with secrets and obsessions. A Mutable square is more flexible, based on other aspects of the chart.

Squares are said to possess a hard energy. Conflict is at their core. A square sets up obstacles and teaches lessons. Despite the tension and conflict, a square can also offer you an opportunity to overcome adversity and to grow.

5

WHEN YOU ARE BORN AND TAKE THAT FIRST BREATH, YOU INGEST THE UNIVERSE, AND THAT IS WHAT LEAVES ITS MARK. HOWEVER, REMEMBER THAT YOUR CHART IS LIKE ANY OTHER MAP. IT'S A WAY TO TRAVEL, BUT YOU DON'T HAVE TO FOLLOW IT. STAY TRUE TO YOUR MISSION, REGARDLESS OF WHAT THE MAP SAYS.

—Fearless Astrology

hat's what I had to do. My mission was to keep that internship. Although it wouldn't make me miss Jeremy any less, it would help me continue my ties to Henry Jaffa. That connection seemed to be the only one that had survived the summer. No, I couldn't allow such negative thoughts into my brain. There had to be a reason Jeremy hadn't gotten in touch with me lately. He had said that he was going to be doing some traveling with his dad. Maybe that's what they were doing. Maybe he'd lost or broken his phone. Maybe.

In the meantime, I decided to start writing an astro love column for *CRUSH*, as if I already had the job. It would be about how to make a Sun fall for you. Once I proved myself to Stacy, I'd have all of these cool columns ready to go. Researching and writing it might even help me figure out how to get Jeremy interested again.

Snider was alone in the classroom that morning, bent over the papers on her desk. As usual, her hair was pulled back, with little curls around her neck. She had lightened it, or maybe just spent some time in the sun. Definitive Capricorn, made even more elegant by the white shirt with high neckline and pearl buttons.

"Good morning," she said, and I could sense her caution.

"I wanted to come in early because I have good news," I told her. "*CRUSH* magazine is going to do a spring issue on beaches next year, and they're coming here to do a photo shoot."

She put down her pen and gave me the first genuine smile I'd seen from her in a long time. "That's wonderful, Logan. How did you make it happen?"

I felt myself flush. "Stacy, the *CRUSH* editor, liked the idea of featuring a beach in a small town."

"So do I. I'm really happy to see you making such positive progress with your internship, Logan."

Probably not a good time to mention that I was trying out

for the teen astrology columnist position. I would worry
about that if and when I got the job.

"I'm excited about it. They'll be picking one model from
here. Can you believe it?"

"Only one?"

"One from each beach community high school. From all
over the country."

"How can we possibly select one?" Snider asked. "I can't
even imagine the wars that will start."

"There won't be any wars," I told her. "Stacy says they are
going to ask the fashion designer featured in that issue to
make the final decisions."

"Which designer?"

"Her name is Graciela Perez. Stacy said she's the hottest
beachwear designer in the country."

"And no astrology?" Although she was still smiling, I knew
it wasn't a joke.

"Just swimsuits, Ms. Snider. No astrology."

At least not right now.

⁂

I knew Snider was going to be a problem if I got the
column, but that couldn't stop me. Stacy was already
beginning to have confidence in me. Even though she had
claimed the beach idea as her own, she was rewarding me by
letting Terra High be one of the featured schools.

The news spread. Other students asked me about it. That day, it seemed as if every girl on campus wanted to be in *CRUSH*. I wondered how that would feel—to know you looked so fabulous that you could be in a national magazine. Or to at least think you could be. If I had that much self-confidence, there would be no stopping me. I might just have the nerve to reach for my phone and call Ireland. Might just demand to know why a certain hot guy had suddenly gone so cold.

"Hi, Chili. Hi, Paige. Hiiii, Logan." Dina Coulter, cheerleader—Kat's Virgo friend, and suck-up, had oily dark hair and bright lips curved into a perpetual valentine smile. In addition to being a royal pain, she spent her days walking the halls and greeting everyone by name. Except for me. We hadn't spoken since I had used astrology to figure out that crazy situation last spring, when I was still a sophomore. But it appeared that I was suddenly once again worthy of attention.

"Hi," the three of us murmured in unison.

"I heard about *CRUSH*," she said, and turned her beady little gaze on me.

"Oh, you did? Are you interested in trying out?"

Chili and Paige rolled their eyes.

"Maybe." Dina shrugged. "I just wanted the guidelines, that's all."

For Kat, of course. Virgo Dina thought there should be a ten-page printed list of rules for everything including getting out of bed in the morning.

"Just show up," I said. "The photographers will be here on Thursday."

"Are there going to be tryouts?"

"No, this isn't cheer. They're just going to take photos at the beach and around the school."

"Come on, Logan," she said. "You've got to have more information than that."

"If I did, I'd tell you, even though I know who you're really asking for."

"So what?" she said. "Kat has as good a chance as any of your friends. That's the real reason you're not sharing what you know, isn't it? You want Chili to get it."

"That's ridiculous," Chili said. "If you think Logan would cheat for me, or if I'd even want her to . . ."

"I wouldn't put anything past either one of you."

"Just a minute," I said before their exchange turned into a fight. "I have no idea who's going to be selected, okay? I was able to get the magazine to feature our school, that's it. And I was lucky to do that."

"Okay then." Dina shrugged and pushed her hair out of her eyes. "I guess we'll just have to wait until Thursday."

With that, she took off down the hall.

"Can you believe her?" Chili said. "She's acting like there's some secret code or something."

"You don't need a secret code to get chosen," I told her.

Paige grinned. "Not if those people at that magazine have a brain among them."

"They do," I said. "But they aren't the ones making the decision. It's the designer who will be featured in the issue. She's going to be at the launch party too."

"What designer?" Paige demanded.

"She does swimsuits. Her name is . . ."

"Not Graciela Perez?"

"Yes, that's the one. Is she good?"

"Oh, Logan," Paige said, "she's awesome! You've got to get me into that party."

"Get us both in." Chili wrapped her arm around me.

"I will do my best," I said. "In the meantime, show up on Thursday in something sexy, both of you."

"What about you?" Paige asked.

"I'll be there to cheer you on," I said. "Astrologer to the stars."

Chili stared at me for a moment, and I knew that it was one of the rare times she wasn't speaking what was on her mind. "Why don't you both come by my house this afternoon? Help me try to figure out what to wear on Thursday."

"I need to get home," I said.

"You can check your e-mail from my computer."

"I know, but I just feel I should be there."

Paige and Chili exchanged looks. "Okay then. We can go through my closet tomorrow." Chili's smile was brighter than ever, and absolutely fake. I was grateful for it just the same.

NOTES TO SELF

My two best friends are worried about me, I can tell. They don't ask about Jeremy anymore, but I know they guessed that I wanted to be home in case he called here, which he never has. That's not really the reason, though. I just know I'm going to hear from him today, and I don't want to be around anyone when I do. In the meantime, I am going to see what I can do about getting them into the *CRUSH* costume party. And I am going to practice writing about crushes for what I hope will be my new column.

CRUSHES: HOW TO SNAG AN ARIES

By Logan McRae

If you want an Aries to notice you, you need to stand out. But not in a trashy way. Showing off your belly button piercing is going to send him a one-word message—"Easy." The been-there-done-that Fire sign is looking for more of a challenge. Here are three ways to give him what he's looking for.

• Hang with other guys. They can be just friends, but they are still going to bring out that Aries competition gene. Meet his eyes and smile over your shoulder as you pass by.

• **Take up a cool sport.** *Aries loves activity. Train for a marathon. Organize a bike trip. Invite some of those male friends of yours.*

• **Is there a cause you believe and are involved in?** *A driving ambition for school or career? Are you the first to volunteer or campaign? Pure Aries bait! The Ram is passion all the way, and he can't help being attracted to a passionate girl. No couch potatoes for this guy.*

What to say when he asks you out: "As a matter of fact, I think I am free that night."

6

LOVING AN EARTH SIGN USUALLY MEANS YOU WILL BE
TOGETHER FOREVER. EVEN A RARE CHEATING EARTH
SIGN WILL TRY TO STICK WITH BOTH LOVE INTERESTS
INDEFINITELY. IF YOU HAVE PICKED A TAURUS, VIRGO, OR
CAPRICORN PARTNER, YOU ARE PROBABLY SET FOR LIFE.
SOMETIMES EVEN MORE SET THAN YOU'D LIKE TO BE.

—Fearless Astrology

```
miss u too
keep in touch
     j
```

was right. I heard from Jeremy. His text showed up
about the time that I got home. My chest felt tight and
ready to explode. Was this the only response he could send

me? What had happened to *I love you*? And what did *keep in touch* mean?

Admit it. I was losing him, losing the guy I loved. He was all I thought about that week, although I didn't mention it to Chili or Paige. Why had Jeremy fallen out of love with me? Had he met someone else? Had he forgotten about how it had been with us? I guess he had. I couldn't give up, though, in spite of everything that was happening right now. I needed to do something to get him to at least talk to me.

As the news continued to spread through Terra High that *CRUSH* would be doing a photo shoot on campus, Kat made it clear that she was determined to be the Terra High model—and so did Chili.

"If only because Kat is so irritating," Chili said as we went through her closet Tuesday after school. "I don't even care that much. But if I don't try, she might actually win."

Stella, Chili's mom, stepped into the room.

"Absolutely nothing that shows cleavage, honey," she announced. "I mean that, Jessica."

She always called Chili by her real name.

"The magazine people are just doing group shots this trip," I said. "They want to see us the way we look at school."

"Your jean skirt with the gathered waist." Paige's eyes gleamed, and she went into Pisces creative mode. "Wear it with your plaid shirt, and your navy striped sweater."

"I don't want them to think I'm trying too hard." Chili turned from the closet of endless possibilities.

"That's the point," I said. "Kat certainly will be trying too hard. You need to do the same."

"Who cares if she does get it? She doesn't have anything else going for her."

"But she's an Aries, and she is going to play every angle," I said. "You know how she is, and she super hates you because you stole her boyfriend last spring."

"For what? About five minutes. She can have him now."

She was such a Gemini.

"Just be sure that you pull down the shirt sleeves from the arms of your sweater, Chili." Paige moved past us into the closet. "It's a really good look. And, Logan, in return for all of this fashion advice, I'd love a personal introduction to the Platinum Dragon."

"Who's that?" I asked.

"Graciela Perez. That's what they call her, and when you see her, you'll understand why."

Now I was starting to get it. "So she's to you what Henry Jaffa is to me?"

"Not even close." She emerged from the closest carrying Chili's jean skirt and several shirts and sweaters. "You and Jaffa are friends. I just want to meet Graciela, that's all. It will totally make my life."

"If I can get Stacy to agree, you're in."

That Thursday, Chili showed up in the striped sweater, red-plaid shirt, and jean skirt. With multi-clustered chandelier earrings, she would be hard to miss when the magazine people got there.

Paige wore white cropped pants with silver zippers at the

pockets and a draped-knit pale blue top in the same shade as her eyes.

"You look great," Chili said when I got into the car beside her. "Isn't that green perfect for her, Paige?"

"Really nice. I love vertical stripes and ruffles on a shirt."

They were lying, trying to make me feel better and probably well aware of my red-rimmed eyes.

"Okay," I said. "So this isn't my best day in the world."

"Here." Paige leaned forward and handed me her cup of coffee. "What happened, Logan?"

"It's Jeremy. He . . ." I couldn't finish. Just held onto that cup that was so much warmer than my hands.

"I knew it," Chili said. "Didn't I tell you, Paige? Didn't I say there was no way it could work out with Logan here and that guy in Ireland?"

"I don't think this is the appropriate time to discuss what we talked about," Paige said, "and Jeremy does have a name. He isn't just *that guy*."

"Right. That's what I meant." Chili turned around and gave me that smile that owned the universe and just assumed that I could too. "But, come on. This really is the appropriate time to talk about what happened with Jeremy that upset you so much. Isn't it, Logan?"

"Probably," I said. "His last text made it pretty clear that he's no longer into me." I spoke clearly, and to my surprise, without tears. Yet my heart felt so dead, so betrayed, that I was certain it would never recover.

"So much for that jerk," Chili said. "At least, Sol is really into you. I already checked out his sign. Cancers are loyal to the end."

"I'm far from the end," I told her, "and I can't exchange men like underwear." *The way you can, Gemini.*

"I'm not suggesting that. All I'm saying is that Sol is hella smart, and he likes you. Can't you at least think about it?"

"I really can't."

"Why not?"

"I don't know."

But I did know. I was still in love with Jeremy.

A guy who said he loved me. A guy who left for Ireland and didn't bother to keep in touch *after the new wore off,* as my Gram would say. Maybe the new had worn off for him, but it hadn't for me. I liked Sol. He was steady and sweet. But he was nothing more to me. No way could I ever feel anything but friendship for him. Could I?

⁓⁓⁓⁓

As we got out of the car, I realized that the photographer was already there. An older guy in glasses, he smiled as we walked toward the classrooms. Next to him was Bobby, the art director, in baggy beige shorts rolled up to his pudgy knees.

Out of nowhere, a shrieking figure in front of me shot into the air.

"Terra High, Terra High. Can't hold us down. We're gonna fly." Kat, of course, in her navy and gold cheer attire. Dina was right behind her in cutoffs. Under each arm was one of those cheesy little exercise steps. Were they really going to build a mini cheer platform out here in the parking lot?

"Later, hon," Bobby said with a bored expression. "These are location shots. We'll get you after school on the beach. Hey, Logan, come over here, and bring your girlfriends."

Kat shot me a nasty look.

Beside her, Dina said, "Hi, Logan. Hi, Paige. Hi, Chili." Her oily hair had actually been washed and run through some kind of flatiron from hell. Her eyes were so heavily lined that they looked like two holes burned in a blanket.

If *CRUSH* obsession had taken over Dina, it must have taken over the entire school. I couldn't wait to get home and away from all of it. But I couldn't. After our last class that day, we were told to show up on the beach, which was about five minutes away. Kat was the first one I saw. She was dressed in a red top-heavy bikini, cut up high on the butt. Mine was blue retro tie-dye and not very revealing, since I didn't have much to reveal. Paige had designed her own with lots of ruffles on the aqua top that would have been flat without them. Chili was perfect in her leopard print that matched the shiny streaks in her hair.

"Line up, will you?" Bobby shouted. "We need you to spell out the word, *CRUSH*. Move your arms and hands so that you resemble the letters. We might actually get this in the magazine, people. Then, you'll all be there."

We managed to do it, and the photographer grinned. "You kids are perfect. Now I'm going to do some individual shots.

Don't let it bother you. Just act the way you always do."

"Terra High, Terra High." Kat began jumping on the higher of the two steps they had set up. Dina clapped her hands in rhythm.

"Um, let's try another group shot," the photographer said. "Line up, please."

Kat and Dina ran in front of him, and Chili wasn't far behind.

"You go too," I told Paige.

"Only if you do."

"Hey, cutie," Kat said to the photographer, "Can I be in the front row for this photo?"

He seemed to consider it.

"Bobby," I called out. "Where are you?"

"Right here, hon."

The art director lumbered over. "What do you need?"

I pointed at Chili and Paige, each of them on either side of me. They grinned up at him.

"I'd like him to take their photos," I said.

He nodded. "I agree. Hey, Ron, get over here."

"Thanks," I said.

Chili tossed her hair and flashed him a smile.

"Work that hair, Chili," Kat yelled. "It's all you've got."

She moved the steps in front of us and began jumping up and down on the higher one, her skirt almost around her waist.

"Terra High, Terra High. We can flyyyyyy."

I'd had it. At the moment she jumped from her perch, I kicked the other step out of the way. With a shriek, she landed on her butt in the sand.

"Go for it, Kat," I said. "Terra High yourself."

NOTES TO SELF

It was my only moment of pleasure that entire day. Never invite an unevolved Aries to a photo shoot. This one got what she wanted, but not the way she had planned. While she swore and whined about her skinned knee, the magazine people ignored her, and Chili happily took out her phone and snapped the scene. She put it on her YUTalk page, and even I had to laugh. I'm home again, trying to figure out how to get the astro column at the magazine and get my guy back. Not much hope there. I've been reading the text again and again, trying to find some kind of rhythm and make some kind of sense from it.

miss u too

keep in touch

j

Could I hate my life any more right now?

CRUSHES: HOW TO TEMPT A TAURUS
By Logan McRae

The Bull is ruled by Venus, which means that he has an appreciation of sensual pursuits, and not just the one all guys are thinking about. Jealousy won't work. Tramp by with another guy, and the Taurus of your dreams will shrug and wander off. Brazenly approaching him isn't the best idea either. He doesn't like surprises, secrets, or games. Screechy cheerleader voices turn him off. His senses rule.

Here are three ways to arouse his interest:

• **Wear classic styles and colors, especially blue and brown, if they look good on you.** *Choose soft, tactile fabrics that say, "Touch me." Use a shower gel that leaves just an intriguing hint of fragrance that will linger as you walk by or lean over to ask him a question.*

• **If you're involved in a class discussion, listen to his opinion.** *This is one guy who's going to be tough to change. Decide from the onset how similar you are before you decide to date him.*

• **Mention the concert you attended last week.** *Talking music, art, and food are sure ways to make him look at you in a new way.*

What to say when he asks you out: *"I know a great little place for dinner."*

7

IF YOU DOUBT THE POWER OF THE MOON, THINK
ABOUT ITS EFFECT ON WATER. EARTH IS 80 PERCENT
WATER, AND THE MOON PULLS THE TIDE. OUR BODIES
HAVE THE SAME MAKEUP. AS ANY LAW ENFORCEMENT
OR EMERGENCY ROOM PROFESSIONAL CAN ATTEST, A
FULL MOON MEANS BEDLAM. AND IF IT HAS THAT KIND
OF EFFECT ON US, IMAGINE WHAT THE REST OF THE
PLANETS CAN DO.

—Fearless Astrology

The moon was full Thursday night. Gemini Moon, good for
communication skills, and I was going to need all the help
I could get. The next morning, a silver shadow of it still
remained in the sky as I drove to San Francisco. Stacy had

asked me to meet her for coffee, and her e-mail had sounded friendly. She'd even signed it "Stace."

We met outside her office. As always, she looked perfect. The black hair made her skin seem even more pale and delicate. Today her dark eyes were lined in turquoise, the same color as the stones in her silver pendant. She looked like the "after" in a makeover photo.

I hoped this was a positive meeting, but with the full moon, I wasn't counting on it.

"Thanks for coming so early, Logan." Her smile was carefully composed as if she were waiting to go on stage. Again, I wondered if she was a Leo. More than that, I wondered what was going on that made it necessary for me to show up ahead of anyone else.

"It was a great drive," I said, only partially lying. "I got to watch the sun come up while the moon was still in the sky."

"Is that helpful for your astro stuff?" She began walking, and I did the same.

"Oh, no. Astrology isn't only about what's going on in the sky. It's also understanding what was going on the moment you were born and figuring out how you've progressed and how you can deal with challenges and successes right now."

"Well put." It was a Henry Jaffa term. In my short association with him, I had learned that it usually meant: *Boring beyond belief. Please shut up.*

"Love your outfit." She checked me out from gray knit cap to skinny jeans. "You're a cute girl, Logan, and you'd be even cuter if you did a little more with your eyes." The *you'd-be-*

even-cuter line reminded me of Chili when she tried to get Paige to wear more makeup. Was that what Stacy wanted to talk to me about? My appearance?

"Thanks. I'm afraid that I'm not very good at that."

"I didn't mean to sound critical."

"Not at all," I said. "I appreciate it." So it wasn't my appearance. What then?

We walked down Columbus toward a building with a glass front, a coffee shop that appeared local rather than Starbuckized. Through the expansive windows, I could see people huddled at tables in a well lit interior of yellow and brown.

"Caffe Greco," I said, reading the sign.

"Order whatever you'd like." She seemed impatient. My stomach was in such a tight knot that I didn't dare eat anything.

"Just a decaf," I said.

The guy at the counter was a cute Latino with rectangular glasses that made his eyes appear enormous.

"Hi, Carlos," she said. "Beautiful day, isn't it? A decaf for her and the usual for me, please."

"Working hard?" He winked.

"Very hard, and I need the coffees to go," she said, her tone clipped. One moment she'd been friendly to him. Now she seemed indifferent. Something was on her mind, all right, and I had a nasty feeling that I was the something.

"Sure thing," he said with a shrug. "We'll get your orders right away."

We walked outside with our drinks. Although I was afraid to speak, Stacy seemed to be having a more difficult time. I stopped on the sidewalk and tried to make eye contact with her.

"So what's going on?"

"The launch party is shaping up well." She took a sip from her cup, as if grateful to avoid looking back at me. "Alex Keen will be catering. We just got that confirmed."

The hot Canadian chef Chili adored. I couldn't wait to tell her about that, but I couldn't think about it right now.

"That's great."

"And Arianna Woods has demanded your dismissal."

"What?" I should have expected this after my run-in with her.

"I'm sorry, Logan. It was really wrong for me to tell her that you shared what she was doing on that social networking page of hers. So, yes, she hates you. And she's trying to get us to terminate your internship."

"Are you going to fire me?" I asked.

"Of course not. Henry would kill me."

So Jaffa was the reason I had my internship. I'd already guessed that. Now I *knew* it.

"What do I have to do to convince her to leave me alone?" I asked.

Stacy lifted her cup to her lips but didn't drink. "Just one thing."

"What?" I asked again.

"You need to try to talk to her," she said. "As you know, she's dealing with a lot right now, but she's coming back with a new CD. It will be awesome when that coincides with our cover."

"Does what Arianna want determine what happens to me?" I asked.

"Not really." She stopped to take another sip. "But kind of."

"What does that mean?"

"That she could go over my head. I don't know that she will. We get along pretty well."

"Would you talk to her about me? Tell her I wasn't trying to cause trouble for her?"

"I already have," she said. "Apparently, she was really attached to her YUTalk page. She feels it was the only way she could be herself with her fans. When we told her people that the magazine deal depended on changing it, she was understandably pissed."

Furious and vengeful was more like it. The very worst swing of the double-edge Gemini sword.

"What could I even say to her? She's a star and I'm just a high school kid."

"That might work to your advantage." She stopped at the crosswalk and gave me a thoughtful look. "I told her that you were sweet and nice, and, well, young."

"And you think that will convince her not to hate me for telling you about the site?"

"Anyone could have done that. And should have." Her expression changed, and I wondered who in the office hadn't followed through on that one. My guess was Danielle, the assistant. "Arianna just needs to see that you're not mean. She can be moody, and for all we know, might have already regretted what she said."

No use in telling her that a Gemini neither regrets nor forgets.

"Do you think she'll actually talk to me?"

She nodded. "That's why I wanted to meet early, so that you'd be prepared."

"Thanks for going to bat for me, Stacy."

"Call me Stace." She smiled. "We'd better jam, though. Arianna's waiting for us back at the office."

NOTES TO SELF

Here I was worried about how to land an astrology column, and now I'm practically begging to keep my job. Fortunately, Arianna is running late, so I have a few minutes to recover before she gets here. I pretend to be cheerful and willing to assist, and there is plenty of work. I can tell by the way Bobby and Mary Elizabeth are treating me that they are unaware of what's going on. Bobby tells me I have cute friends, and Mary Elizabeth compliments me on my "fab little beanie."

Now, I have a minute to check out *Fearless Astrology*. I've learned that it's a good idea to keep it handy at all times. I never know when I need some fast advice. This is one of those times.

8

ANGER IS A SECONDARY EMOTION, AND NEVER MORE
TRUE THAN IN THE CASE OF GEMINI. A CAR RUNS A
STOPLIGHT AND HEADS FOR YOU. YOU HONK THE HORN.
YOU SMASH YOUR THUMB WITH A HAMMER, AND YOU
SWEAR. IN BOTH CASES, ANGER IS THE SECONDARY
EMOTION. THE CAR SCARED YOU. THE HAMMER HURT
YOU. REMEMBER THIS WHEN DEALING WITH WHAT
APPEARS TO BE AN ANGRY GEMINI. LOOK FOR WHAT IS
UNDERNEATH THAT ANGER.

—Fearless Astrology

I reminded myself that Arianna was a Gemini Air sign.
When I met with her in Stacy's office, I tried to decide
what her primary emotion was. But she didn't look afraid or

hurt. She just looked angry. The multicolored hair was pulled back, giving her navy eyes a feline slant that only made her appear more unfriendly.

She wore jeans and a little lacy white shirt that was too thin for the unpredictable weather outside. Not to mention, too revealing. Although she was less than five years older than I, there was a world of experience between us. She slouched in her chair and looked across at me from time to time, as if I were a bug she'd like to crush with that chunky sandal of hers.

"Well," Stacy said, "Today it's my turn to get the coffee." What a joke. She just wanted to ditch the office and us as soon as possible, leaving me to deal with Arianna by myself.

"Red Bull for me." She looked as if she needed it. Her speaking voice had a husky, cheerleader quality that didn't sound anything like her singing one.

Stacy met my eyes and then turned away quickly and closed the door behind her.

"So?" Arianna picked at a white nail tip.

"Well," I began, my voice shaking. "I appreciate that you're willing to talk to me."

"Like I had a choice?"

"I mean . . ." This was worse than I had imagined. " . . . I really didn't realize that what you had on your YUTalk page was secret."

"Dude. It wasn't secret, but nobody important bothered checking it out until you opened your kiss-ass mouth."

"I didn't know I was doing anything wrong," I said.

"So you ratted me out, just like that. And you royally pissed off the magazine people, Stacy included. Don't tell me you didn't know that would happen."

"I didn't know," I said. "This internship means everything to me. Do you really think I'd do something as stupid as that to jeopardize it?"

"Being able to say whatever I wanted on that blog, it was like having someone to talk to." She jumped out of her chair, and it was as if someone had flipped an invisible energy switch. "Why can't I ever just have someone to freakin' talk to?"

She stalked to the window as if no longer aware of me. Afraid or hurt? I was guessing both.

"Communication is everything to a Gemini," I said softly. "You have to have it. You must."

She whipped around to face me. "How the hell do you know I'm a Gemini?"

"Your birthday is on your YUTalk page."

"Oh, right. But what made you think of communication? How'd you know that?"

"I'm kind of into astrology," I said. "I also have a good friend who's a Gemini."

"Does she have man problems, too?"

I forced a laugh, tried to sound relaxed. "Make that *men* problems. Good song material, though."

"Don't even go there." She returned to her chair and began picking at her nails again. "Cory wrote the songs. Everyone knows that."

"I hear what you're saying," I told her, and hoped it

connected to her Air sign core. "Gemini is ruled by Mercury. You're all about delivering information."

"How do I know you're not just making that up?" she asked.

"Check any astrology site. Gemini is an information junkie, but can quickly lose interest in any project or person. Their cure for a challenging love relationship is to have someone else on the back burner."

That got a smile out of her. "You're pretty good."

"Basic Gemini Sun stuff," I said, and realized that *Fearless Astrology* just might be saving my internship for me. "If I knew where your other planets were, then I could really get specific."

"What would you need to find out that stuff?"

Of course I already knew it, but I couldn't tell her I did.

"For your Moon, Mercury, Mars, and Venus, just your birthday." *Which I already had, thank you very much.* "For your Rising sign and houses, I need your time and place of birth."

"You really don't make this stuff up, do you?"

"No," I said. "Just don't ask me how it works, because I don't have a clue. And it doesn't mean you're locked into only one way of behaving or any one outcome."

"You sure about that?" She finally stared into my eyes, and there was so much sadness in her expression that I almost forgot that the purpose of this conversation was to save my job.

"Absolutely sure. The stars only point out potential and possibilities. They don't limit you." Now I was starting to sound like *Fearless Astrology*. Had I said too much and made her think I was too out there?

"Just so you know. It gives me no pleasure whatsoever to go around bullying an intern. But sometimes I just get so pissed."

That anger again.

"I can't imagine what it must be like for you," I said. "For that matter, I can't even believe I'm in the same room with you. My best friend loves your music so much that she plays it every day to and from school."

For a moment, she tried to smile, then seemed to give up on it. "Honey, you have no idea."

I wanted to ask *no idea about what*, but it was clear that I had no idea about anything in her world. But I was *honey* now, and that might just mean she wasn't going demand that I be fired.

"Well, if you ever want me to do your chart . . ." I began.

". . . With that hair, I'll bet there's a lot of Fire there." As if I didn't know.

NOTES TO SELF

Stacy (make that Stace) never returned to her office that morning. Arianna got even more jittery and distracted. Yet we were able to talk through our differences and finally stood at Stacy's window overlooking the trees beneath the office.

I still have my internship. Although Arianna didn't say it, I know that she is no longer interested in punishing me. Here's the problem. I kind-of sense something decent in her beneath the glitter and the blond-gold red hair extensions.

Now I have to shift back into high school mode. Who would believe that I actually met with the real Arianna? Who would believe that beneath her fury was something far sadder? No one I know, that's for sure.

9

LOVE BRINGS OUT THE WORST—AND BEST—IN EVERY
SIGN. FIRE SIGNS (ARIES, LEO, SAGITTARIUS) EITHER
CHALK UP ANOTHER CONQUEST OR VOW TO CHANGE
THEIR WANDERING WAYS. EARTH SIGNS (TAURUS, VIRGO,
CAPRICORN) MIGHT EITHER TRY TO IMPRISON THE
OBJECT OF DESIRE OR RELINQUISH CONTROL IN RETURN
FOR MUTUAL COMMITMENT. AIR SIGNS (GEMINI, LIBRA,
AQUARIUS) MAY DRIFT AWAY WHEN THE LOVED ONE
APPEARS DISINTERESTED. OR THEY MAY USE THEIR
CONSIDERABLE COMMUNICATION SKILLS TO OVERCOME
THEIR FEAR OF RISK. WATER SIGNS (CANCER, SCORPIO,
PISCES) WILL DECIDE IF THEY WANT TO SETTLE FOR OR
SETTLE DOWN. WHAT ONE DECIDES TO DO IN LOVE
FREQUENTLY DEPENDS ON HOW MUCH ONE IS IN LOVE.

—Fearless Astrology

I wasn't sure how "considerable" my communication skills were, but I did know this Air sign must overcome the risk of hearing that Jeremy no longer loved me. I had to know the truth, even if it was as horrible as I was starting to suspect. By Monday, I still had no word from him. I couldn't just keep hoping something would change. I had to make it change, if I could. I had to risk.

In chemistry class that morning, I decided to text him again and make it clear how much I needed to hear the truth. I couldn't wait any longer, but I had to be careful. Bodmer was sharp. She had even caught Paige texting, which was almost impossible to do. With that glazed Pisces look, Paige could stare straight ahead and sneak one hand into her bag. Fortunately, she didn't have to go to the SRC, where most of those caught committing texting crimes ended up.

The Student Responsibility Center, better known as the Stupid Rules Center, was Terra Bella High's River Styx, and it divided our normal world from the underworld of the dreaded vice principal, Dr. West. Once delivered there, students were examined for dress code violations. Was a T-shirt a solid color, thus suggesting a gang affiliation? Violation! Was there a team name or symbol on it? A hole in someone's jeans? Did shoes reveal too much flesh? Violation, violation, violation! Phones were kept until claimed by parents. Detention ruled. But I was getting ready to risk it all with my phone just then.

Bodmer limited her talking time to ten minutes max. Which meant I had exactly that much time to tell Jeremy what I must say to him. Still in lecture mode, she was speaking about the relationship between mass and moles. Not the on-your-body-type moles. A mole, as she loved to point out, was just an easy way of counting atoms.

After doing a couple of problems on the board, she stopped, glanced around the room with her hawk eyes, and lifted a brown bag of candy. "In this lab, we will use M&Ms." She stared right at me as if she knew I had something else on my mind.

"Ms. Bodmer?" Dina raised her hand. "Yes, Dina?"

"Could we go over the procedure again?"

"We discussed it in the last class." Bodmer made eye contact with me. "Can anyone explain?"

Not my first priority. I needed to get in touch with Jeremy. I'd played the head-trip Aquarius for too long already. My phone was in my bag. Slowly, I reached down, then slid it into my lap. Then I moved my book to the edge of the desk. That would hide what I was doing.

"Logan?"

"We're supposed to count the candy, and then determine the volume and mass," I said.

"And why are we using M&Ms in this lab?" Why wouldn't she leave me alone? Dina turned and shot me that tacky valentine smile.

"Is it because it's easier that way to visualize the size of a mole?" I asked.

She nodded. "Why is that?"

"Because M&Ms are much bigger than atoms?"

"Exactly." At least she seemed satisfied with my answer.

Finally, she turned her attention to the class. "Three moles of water would fill about two ounces, not quite a quarter cup. That's how small they are."

Then she returned to the board and was so busy trying to make her point, that I finally had an opportunity to text Jeremy. The friendly *how-you-doings* were behind us. I needed to tell him the truth now.

> J: do u still love me?
> Need to know
> I still love u

"Logan, are you with us?" I looked up into Bodmer's steady gaze. How long had she been watching me? As I did so, I realized that in addition to the glasses she was wearing, she had two more pushed into her hair. "Tell me what three moles of M&Ms will fill."

Dina's hand shot up, but Bodmer continued to look at me. I could take a wild guess or tell the truth.

"I'm not sure," I said. So much for my *considerable communication skills.*

Dina gave me a pathetic smile. "It's right up there on the board," she said, as if trying to be helpful. "About three moles of M&Ms would completely fill the oceans of the world." She wasn't trying to make points with Bodner, only driving the knife into me. A Virgo tactic, for sure.

Bodmer ignored her. I was getting The Look, and the rest of the class knew it. Slowly, all heads turned toward me.

"So, what's in your lap?" Bodmer asked, in that flippant way that made it clear she already knew the answer.

"My phone," I said, "but I wasn't . . ."

She put out her hand. "Give it to me."

"But I wasn't . . ."

"You know the rules, Logan. Just hand it over. And the rest of you had better be smart enough to have yours put away. If you don't, I'll have to take them too."

The rest of class was a blur. I just knew that Jeremy was texting me back, and I had no way of knowing. No way of even getting back to him.

I waited after class and finally approached Bodmer at the door.

"Sorry about what happened today," she said, before I could speak. "By the way, don't ever take up poker. Your face gives you away."

"I've never tried to text in your class before," I told her. "If so, you would have caught me."

"That's for sure." She shoved a mass of curls behind her ear, and I saw a large dangling earring that was as out there as the leopard print glasses on her head.

That reminded me again that, although she gave some of the hardest tests I'd ever taken, she wasn't a by-the-rules teacher.

"Since I've never done it before, could you give me a second chance?" I asked.

She shook her head. "I'm required to take away phones from kids who use them inappropriately. You know that."

"You're not going to send it to the SRC, are you?"

"Of course not," she said.

"Thank you."

"You messed up," she said, "but you only messed up once. I'll just keep it in my drawer while you have time to think about why you should not text in class."

"But I need it," I told her. "Please, could you make an exception, just this time?"

"I already made one, and a big one, at that. I'm not turning it over to the vice principal." She returned to her desk, opened the drawer and put my phone inside. "It will be waiting for you here next Monday."

Monday? "Please," I said. "I can't be without a phone that long. It's really important."

"It's really important that you pay attention in class, and you can't do that if you're only pretending to listen." She sat on the edge of her desk and gave me a friendly grin as if trying to make me understand that she was helping instead of destroying me. "I know you have a lot going on right now with your magazine internship, and that's okay. What you did today is not."

"I know that, but I have to be in San Francisco Friday morning. I can't go without my phone. What if I got in an accident or something? What if I got sick and had to call home?"

"I get your point." She stood up, and for a moment, I thought she was going to reach for the drawer, and give it back to me. "I've been known to break a rule now and then," she said. "Tell you what. Stop by Thursday afternoon, and I'll let you have it." She glanced up at the clock. "Anything else I can do for you today, Logan?"

NOTES TO SELF

I had been brave enough to text Jeremy and demand the truth. Now, I won't be able to read his answer. If there is an answer. If he cares enough to text back.

Later that day, Dina's heart-shaped, over-glossed smile was bigger than ever when she greeted me in the hall with "Hiiii, Logan." Translated: Wait till Kat hears how you blew it in Bodmer's class. I don't care about Kat, though. I care about Jeremy. And I care about the phone I'm not going to have back until Thursday night.

WHERE'S YOUR MERCURY?
By Logan McRae

The location of Mercury in your chart determines your communication style. Mercury, the messenger of the zodiac, also affects intellect, short trips, and everyday learning. In Greek mythology, he was Hermes, son of Zeus, who on the day of his birth stole cattle from his brother, Apollo. When the Greek astronomers were choosing names for the planets, they named the fastest one for Mercury. The ruler of both Gemini and Virgo, this planet also rules writers, salespeople, even magicians. When it shows up in a fiery sign, even shy Sun signs speak with more passion.

Mercury in Aries. *Aries is an action sign. With this placement, you can often speak before you think. You can also be more forceful when you talk, and sometimes bossy.*

Mercury in Taurus. *Taurus is not a chatterbox. Far from it. When Mercury is here, you may have a speaker who talks slowly and who is more deliberate with word choice.*

Mercury in Gemini. *Mercury rules Gemini, and Gemini is at home with words. This placement can make any sign a strong communicator, and in some cases, too much of one.*

Mercury in Cancer. *The Crab often works behind the scenes. When Mercury is in this sign, the speaking style is frequently soft-spoken and sometimes manipulative.*

Mercury in Leo. *The Lion is fond of attention. When Mercury lands there, the communication style will usually be more exuberant.*

Mercury in Virgo. *Mercury rules Virgo as well as Gemini. Since Virgo is all about details, a Merc-Virgo placement can create a communication style that is full of facts, figures, and sometimes, minutiae.*

Mercury in Libra. *These speakers are diplomatic and often good negotiators. The communication style is more balanced (some would say wishy-washy), and the speaker will consider (or appear to consider) both sides of an issue.*

Mercury in Scorpio. *The Scorpion is rooted in the past, and many could live with minimal conversation. Even a chatty Air sign will be more thoughtful and serious with this placement.*

Mercury in Sagittarius. *Sagittarius is ruled by Jupiter, the planet of expansion. When Mercury lands here, it may result in a speaker who is never-ending verbose and nonstop talkative.*

Mercury in Capricorn. *The hardworking Mountain Goat has no time to mince words. The communication style here will be more matter-of-fact, borderline rude, and could appear cold and unemotional.*

Mercury in Aquarius. *Aquarius thinks before speaking. And thinks and thinks. When Mercury resides there, the speaking style can be a little (and probably a lot) on the analytical side.*

Mercury in Pisces. *The Fish slips around instead of through obstacles. You might tend to "think" your great comebacks instead of actually speaking them. You might also talk around a subject without coming to the point.*

10

How assertive are you? You'll find part of the answer in your Sun sign. Fire signs (Aries, Leo, Sagittarius) are the most assertive of all. They blaze ahead without giving a thought as whether or not they are equipped to. If you are a Fire sign, learn to think first. Earth signs (Taurus, Virgo, Capricorn) are more deliberate than assertive. In conflict, they push ahead at their own pace. If you are an Earth sign, learn to listen. Air signs (Gemini, Libra, Aquarius) truly believe they are aggressive, but their power is in words as often as action. If you are an Air sign, learn to not just talk but act. Those conflict-avoiding Water signs (Cancer,

SCORPIO, PISCES) CAN BE THE MOST PASSIVE-
AGGRESSIVE OF ALL. THEY ARE THE ONES WHO SIMMER
SILENTLY, THEN TAKE OUT THEIR ANGER BY PUNISH-
ING THEMSELVES. IF YOU ARE A WATER SIGN, LEARN
TO SPEAK OUT.

—Fearless Astrology

All week, my emotions twisted and turned. Jeremy might be trying to get in contact with me. Sure, my dad and I had a land line at home, but my cell was the number I gave everyone. It was the way Jeremy and I had once connected. The way we might connect again now that it was Thursday, and I had my cell back. There were no messages from him, but four from Stacy.

They were all identical. "Call me when you can."

I tried to reach her Thursday night but got no answer. Worse, I'd be leaving too early the next day for me to return the call. I hoped it was not important.

riday was a teacher in-service, so Chili offered to drive me to San Fran. Stella, her mom, had said we could stay at the Chiliderians' condo in the Embarcadero. She planned to join us that night for dinner and shopping the next day. Having my friends with me made me less nervous than I had been on my previous trips to the magazine office.

Chili drove the streets of San Francisco as if she had been born there. Unlike me, she seemed to sense which ones were one-way and which were dead ends. After some fast corners, and a stomach-clutching ride down a hill, she stopped in front of the building.

"This is the place. How'd you find it?"

"Gemini instinct." She flashed me a grin, and her highlights gleamed in the early morning light. "Now aren't you glad we got here early? Call me when you're finished for the day."

"And have fun." Paige squeezed my shoulder from the backseat. "And, please, please, please ask if you can get us into the party. I've got to meet the Platinum Dragon."

"I'll try," I told her. "See you tonight."

Stacy stood at the office door as I walked in, a black-and-white stenciled bag over the shoulder of her fitted red jacket. "Don't you ever answer your phone?" she asked.

"I'm sorry." No way could I tell her that said phone had been confiscated by my chemistry teacher. "I didn't have it, but I checked my voice mail."

"You know I don't do voice mail," she said. "You could see my number there, and you could have called me back if you'd wanted to. I needed you here early today."

"It is early." I started to get that tight, anxious knot in my stomach again.

"Not really." She glanced at her watch, an asymmetric strip of silver around her tiny wrist. "We're supposed to be at the hotel making plans for the launch party. Do you realize it's in less than a month? I've been trying to get in touch with you for days, Logan. We missed the car. Now we're going to have to get a taxi."

What had Bodmer done to me?

"My friends just dropped me off," I said. "They can't be that far away. I'm sure they can give us a ride."

"You need to call them." She sighed in that obvious way she frequently used to convey her impatience. "I can't waste another minute. After I leave the hotel, I've got to meet Arianna for a photo shoot."

Chili answered immediately. "What's going on?"

"How soon can you get back here?" I asked. "My editor and I need a ride."

"Cool. We're going around the block right now. Get us in, okay?"

"I'll try," I said, and to Stacy, "They're on their way. I'm so sorry I missed your calls."

"As long as we get there before Alex pitches a fit," she said, but her expression was tight and unfriendly.

Before I could try to make any more excuses, Chili pulled up in front of the office. Stacy climbed into the front seat beside her. I got in beside Paige.

"I really appreciate this," Stacy told Chili. "I had hoped to reach Logan earlier. The only time we can work on our launch party is when the hotel isn't busy. The head chef isn't happy, as it is, that we're disrupting his staff's routine."

"No problem." Chili tossed her hair, and I could only imagine the strength of her smile. "We'll get you there."

"Thank you. Alex Keen is our celebrity chef, and he doesn't like to be left waiting."

That was for sure. Keen had been known to walk off any number of events that didn't live up to his top-chef expectations.

I realized that Chili seemed frozen, her fingers gripping the wheel. Paige gave me a little smile. Alex Keen. Our talkative Gemini friend had just gone speechless. Still, she got us to the hotel in minutes. Without asking, she climbed out of the car, and motioned Paige to do the same.

Stacy shot me a look, and I could see the doubt in that refined expression of hers.

"I appreciate the ride," she said to Chili in the tone and attitude she might address a limo driver she wasn't going to tip.

"Could they come with us?" I asked.

"No offense," she said, in a voice that carried nothing but. "I just don't want to walk in there, late, with three high school girls in tow, okay? I mean, Alex would laugh me out of the place. Do you realize the pressure that's on me? I've got to run a new magazine, plan this event, and still come up with a costume of my own for the launch party."

"Paige?" I asked, but her lips seemed stitched shut. "Can't you help?"

"What?" Stacy demanded.

"Paige is really into fashion," I said. "You need something original and creative for the event, right? High school or not, she's the one who can help you design it."

"She can?" Stacy narrowed her eyes, and I could see the panic in Paige's frozen face.

"Most definitely," Chili said. "She's already taking college design classes, and I know she could do the perfect costume for you, if . . ."

"If you let us all go in with you," I finished. Had I actually said that? Better yet, was Stacy actually considering it?

"What type of costume would you suggest?"

"Maybe Queen of Hearts," Paige mumbled. "But you probably already thought of that."

"Hearts, as in *CRUSH*." Stacy's face lit up, and I felt chills. "How would you go about it?"

"I'm not sure. You could go traditional with the high, lacy collar. Or you could take some chances, tart it up a little. Maybe a jeweled velvet choker and low neckline. Yes, the way I'd do it, Ms. Rogers, is . . ."

"Call me Stace," she said.

Paige called her Stace. We all did. And then we started strolling down the street toward the hotel like four best friends. Leave it to the shy Pisces to surprise us all by baiting my editor with the possibility of a Queen of Hearts costume. They walked ahead of Chili and me, Stacy's dark head bent close to Paige's blond one.

"That red is perfect for you," she told Stacy. "Before you

write me off, at least give me a chance to show you what I can do."

Chili started to follow them inside the elevator. I touched her arm and shook my head.

"We'll meet you upstairs," I said, and watched the elevator doors slide shut.

"What are we going to do now?" Chili demanded.

"Give them time together. Have you ever seen Paige that assertive?"

"Never. But she knows what she's talking about. Even that bitch could see it."

"Stacy isn't a bitch," I told her.

"Well, she wasn't exactly friendly in the car."

"She let you in here, didn't she? Come on, the stairs can't be that far away."

"Okay, if you say so." She grinned. "You wouldn't happen to know Alex Keen's sign, would you?"

"He's a Sagittarius. Remember when the food channel celebrated his birthday last December?"

"Only my mom watches that stuff." She stopped and put her hands on her hips. "I see no stairs, Logan."

"We'll find them. In the meantime, want to hear more about Sagittarius?"

"All I want to hear is if he and I would be a good match."

"I don't know about him personally, but Gemini and Sagittarius are opposites. So yes and maybe. Absolutely a better match than that Scorpio you just dumped."

"I am so over him. He never let me know what he was thinking."

"You wouldn't have that problem with a Sadge." I was about to say that she might have the opposite problem when someone called from behind us.

"Girls, wait. Do you know where the service elevator is?"

I turned to see Alex Keen heading toward us pushing a table on wheels. On top of it was some kind of rectangular device that looked like a miniature barbecue.

"Logan." Chili sounded as if she were choking.

"Stay cool," I whispered.

Yes, it really was Alex Keen, looking even younger in person. Big brown eyes, a tumble of blond curls. That cute Canadian lilt to his voice that always sounded as if he were smiling. Which he was.

"The service elevator," he repeated, and stood beside me.

"Down here," I said, as if I knew where I was going. After all, we'd been over the entire building and hadn't seen it. "Come on."

"Are you sure?" he asked. "I'm late as hell, and I hate this city."

"You can't hate San Francisco," I told him, and desperately looked for anything resembling an elevator.

"I don't really, but this is my first time here, and I've been lost since the moment I got off the plane. Hey, what's that door?"

I almost ran right into the wrought-iron gate partially covering it.

"Service elevator." I pulled the gate open and rushed inside, where I found a Hold button and kept my finger on it.

"Finally." Alex gestured to Chili. "Can you help me get this smoker inside?"

"Sure," she said, and they guided it in. I pressed my back

against the wall to make room. Alex and Chili did the same.

"We can go up now. Thanks for helping me. Are you girls with the magazine?"

"Yes," I said, and it didn't even feel like a lie. "I'm Logan McRae. This is Jessica Chiliderian."

"Chili." She clutched the edge of the table. "I love your show," she stammered. "I wish you'd do more with Armenian cooking, though. Our culture doesn't receive the attention it deserves."

"Armenian?" He leaned back even farther against the elevator wall, and I couldn't tell if he was taking in how cute she was or actually thinking about what she had just suggested. "Armenian might be fun."

Just then, the elevator stopped with a sudden jolt.

Chili screamed.

"What's going on?" Alex demanded, as if I had answers. "Where the hell are we?"

I pushed the Open button. Nothing. I pushed the Lobby button. Again, nothing.

"Not sure," I said. "I think we're stuck."

"Oh, Logan." Chili hated small spaces, and I knew that she was terrified. "What are we going to do?"

"Just stay calm." I was nowhere close to that myself. "Look, there's a phone right here."

I took it out and dialed the operator. Not even a dial tone.

"It's dead," I told them. "I can't reach anyone."

"No wonder." Alex lifted the cord. It dangled free in his hand. "Looks like it's been cut. This is clearly vandalism.

Or worse."

I shivered. *Or worse*? "Who knew you'd be here today?" I asked.

"The magazine, my people, and the hotel chef. I told him I was bringing this smoker and couldn't use the regular elevator. I'm already late. If he has any sense, maybe he'll check and find out where we are."

"How would he know?"

"Well, sooner or later someone's going to realize that the elevator isn't moving." He pointed on the glowing numeral on the silver panel. "We're stuck at the eleventh floor."

"At least we're at a floor." I hit the Open button, and received no response. "Maybe there's been a power failure," I said.

"That still doesn't explain this." He lifted the cord again. "It has to be vandalism."

"Maybe. But why? Who would benefit from stopping us at the wrong floor?"

Just then the elevator took a tiny lurch. Chili gasped, and Alex's face seemed to go even more pale.

"If it's broken," he said, "it just won't hang here forever, will it? I mean, if someone doesn't come and figure how to get us the rest of the way up, we could drop back down, couldn't we?"

"From the weight," Chili whispered. "Oh, Logan, your cell."

Right. My wonderful cell, finally back in my possession.

"It probably won't work in here," I said, "but I can try."

I clicked on Stacy's number and heard a blur of conversation.

"Stacy, we need help," I said, trying not to panic.

"Where are you?" Her voice broke up as she spoke.

"The service elevator. We're stuck between floors." And then, because I wanted to impress upon her how urgent this was, I added, "Alex Keen is with us."

"Alex Keen? Oh, no. What are you doing in the service elevator? Don't worry. Tell him I'm handling it. I'll call maintenance at once."

The phone went dead, and I put it back in my bag. "Stacy's working on it," I said.

"It's so creepy." Chili huddled next to Alex. "How long do you think before they get us out of here, Logan?"

"Any second now," I told her, trying to sound confident. But I wasn't liking the way it felt either. The close, still air was stifling, and the table and the contraption on top of it took up most of the space.

"See what I mean?" Alex said. "I hate this city."

"Me too." Chili gave me a guilty look. "At least right now."

"We're going to be okay." I tried to smile but was too scared.

Then the elevator bumped again. Shuddered and groaned. Alex and Chili grabbed onto each other.

Slowly we began moving up. I let out my breath.

The doors slid open, and we rushed out. Paige waited outside.

"I'm so glad you're all right." She put her arm around me and hugged Chili.

Stacy hurried down the hall toward us. "There was no power," she said. "Whoever turned it off for maintenance must have forgotten to turn it back on again. The custodian just flipped a switch, and everything was fine."

"Why would they turn it off for maintenance when the

elevator was between floors?" I asked.

"I don't know. I'm just glad you're okay." She smiled at Alex and put out her hand. "Hi, Alex, I'm Stacy Rogers. It's so good to finally meet you. Do you need some help setting up?"

"Chili's assisting me," he replied, in that charming accent.

Stacy and I exchanged looks, but all she said was, "Fine."

"I brought my new smoker. It's my own design." He pulled it out of the elevator as Chili held the door. "The head chef made it clear I owed him one for using his kitchen."

Alex and Chili rolled the smoker into the kitchen, a large open area adjoining the banquet room.

"This place is enormous." Paige gestured at the dazzling view of the city. Then she looked at me, and her expression grew serious. "Logan, are you okay?"

"Someone cut the phone line in the service elevator," I said.

"Are you sure?" Stacy asked.

"That's what it looks like."

"I'll call the custodian at once. Regardless of the cause, they need to fix it. You guys could have been stuck there for a long time."

She left, and I wandered through the banquet room. The hotel staff, dressed in uniforms of burgundy and gray, went about their jobs in efficient silence. In the kitchen, I could hear Chili chatting up Alex about exotic dishes, Armenian recipes, celebrity chefs, and food styling—subjects I had never before known were of interest to her.

Stacy returned and said that maintenance was checking out the elevator. She gave the hotel staff the impression that Paige and I were her assistants. We made our checklist for the catering manager, and Paige and Stacy continued to discuss the Queen of Hearts costume. As they spoke the language of tulle and hoop petticoats, I tried to look busy and thought about what almost happened on that elevator. Could it have anything to do with the danger the ephemeris had warned of?

A few minutes after we arrived, a rail-thin older guy joined us.

"I'm Francis," he told Stacy, "the executive chef here."

"Francis, hi." Alex walked into the banquet area, Chili behind him. "Here's my menu for the event. I hope you like the smoker." He handed the menu to him, and they stood apart like two matadors confronting each other.

"I appreciate your generosity," the chef said, with no hint of admiration. "It looks state-of-the-art."

"As I recall, Francis, it was part of the bargain for the gracious loan of your kitchen and staff. Besides, I wanted to be sure the salmon for the party is smoked my way. Want me to show you how it works?"

"I think I can figure it out. And of course, I would appreciate your finishing up here as soon as possible," Francis said. "I have a hotel kitchen to run."

"We'll handle it," Alex replied, pleasantly enough, though I still sensed tension between the two of them.

As we started work, I saw why. Francis was the king of this kitchen, but Alex was the star. Francis was in charge of taking the menu Alex gave him and figuring out how to prep it, cook it, and serve it. Alex was the one signing autographs for the staff.

"I need to check out your salamander to be sure the temperature is right for my oysters." Alex shot a critical look at a gleaming drawer above the oven. "My cilantro pesto must sizzle in two minutes, maybe even less time."

"It will sizzle." Francis almost spit the words at him. "We can check the salamander later. I really need you to hurry up now. I hadn't counted on your tardiness today."

"And I hadn't counted on your service elevator screwing up today." He gave the chef an arrogant smile. "But I'm ready to move forward if you are."

As Alex went to work, I could see that he was even more remarkable than he was on television. The simple act of slicing a cucumber—knuckles firm against the flesh as the thin, pale strips fanned out against the cutting board—left even Chili speechless. I had to admit it was amazing, yet I kept thinking about that elevator and the dangling telephone cord.

After we finished walking through the event with the hotel staff and making sure the hotel kitchen could meet the demands of the menu Alex had provided, he and Chili passed out the food samples he had prepared.

"Try this," Alex said to me. "It's not your basic salsa, I promise."

True, watermelon salsa was not my usual breakfast, but Alex Keen wasn't my usual anything. I ate it on a carrot popper and couldn't remember tasting anything more exotic, not even when Chili's mom cooked for me.

"Pretty wonderful, isn't it?" he said with that Sadge laugh.

I swallowed my last bite of the spicy appetizer and couldn't help smiling up at him.

"So you no longer hate San Francisco?"

His gaze moved to Chili again, and those big brown eyes met hers with such intensity that I could feel the sparks from where I stood. "I'm starting to like it better by the moment. And I have every intention of making the most of my time here."

Chili blushed and began clearing the table.

"I need to hurry, though. We're packing a lot into one day. There's a big photo shoot this afternoon."

"That's right. Stacy said she's meeting Arianna Woods there."

"Arianna Woods?" he asked, and his tone was suddenly almost hostile. "What are you talking about?"

"She's the cover model for the first issue. Didn't you know?"

"I don't remember if we discussed it or not. Doesn't matter."

Just then, he reached for the huge tub of ice that held the cold appetizers, yanked it toward him and right off the table. Ice cubes and shrimp rolls bounced in every direction, and the table sailed into the wall.

"Damn," he shouted. "I can't talk while I'm working. And look what happened. Who's going to clean up this mess? Come on, people, I need some help here. This is what I get for traveling without staff."

Chili scrambled into action, and several hotel workers joined her. The famous Alex Keen temper. What had Stacy said? Pitch a fit? He was pitching one, all right.

NOTES TO SELF

So Alex Keen really does have a temper, unusual for a Sadge. And he seemed angry that I brought up Arianna. Sagittarius can be a clumsy sign, but I'm not so sure that was the case. The flying food and ice effectively ended our conversation. I'd really like to get my hands on his chart and see what else is lurking in there. Maybe nothing. And maybe even what happened in the elevator today was one of those weird freak accidents that no one can explain.

THREE OR FOUR TIMES A YEAR, MERCURY, THAT TINY PLANET THAT'S BARELY VISIBLE JUST BEFORE SUNRISE OR JUST AFTER SUNSET, APPEARS TO TRAVEL BACKWARD FOR APPROXIMATELY THREE WEEKS. IT'S CALLED RETROGRADE, AND IT CAN CAUSE US TO TRAVEL BACKWARD AS WELL. FORWARD MOVEMENT MAY BE STRAINED. THIS IS A TIME TO AVOID RUSHING INTO ANY NEW RELATIONSHIPS AND TO EXAMINE PAST DECISIONS. IT'S LIKELY YOU WILL RUN INTO AN OLD LOVE, IN PERSON OR IN A DREAM, DURING THIS PERIOD OF REVERSAL.

—*Fearless Astrology*

already knew all about Mercury in Retrograde. Early this year, my friends and I had lost car keys and phones, and once when we were at the hair salon, Chili's highlights had actually turned orange. The stylist had blamed the new color she was using, but I knew better.

This time, Retrograde would start in Taurus and end in Gemini. That meant communication and relationship issues. If only I could blame Jeremy's silence on the planets. I knew I'd have to phone him and make him tell me what the hell was going on. But that phone call would have to wait. After what had happened in the hotel elevator on Friday, I couldn't sit around obsessing about my love life. The incident proved I was right that day in journalism class when I called up the ephemeris and saw possible danger for someone at the Halloween launch party. What if the stalled elevator wasn't an accident? What if someone had wanted to scare Alex, or worse?

Doing a quick online search for his birth date was easy. What wasn't easy was locating information on the year he was born. In order to get more than a newspaper horoscope for him, I had to find it.

I asked Chili, and she said that, yes, he was twenty-one, but age was only a number. She then asked about how compatible their signs were. I told her that Sadge and Gemini were opposites on the astral wheel, and there as well as most places, opposites attract. I didn't add that the attraction was often temporary, or that Alex Keen was too sophisticated to do more than flirt with someone our age.

Most of the girls at school were extra nice to me that Monday, as if I had the power to get them in *CRUSH*. I felt as phony as Dina and her perpetual frozen smile.

After Kat's little *accident* on the beach, she was back to not speaking to me, which was the only good thing that happened that day.

Chili had to tutor a math student after her last class, so I had driven myself to school because I needed to stay late to help with the newspaper. A bunch of stories had come in past deadline. One was about University of California changing its requirements for freshmen. Another was a warning about the repercussions of students involved in *sexting*, which made me wonder who had gotten caught sending naked pictures this time.

Sol caught up with me in the parking lot. His long hair fell across his face, somehow making him appear even larger than he already was. I looked up at him, those kind blue eyes. Emotional Cancer, I reminded myself, probably had issues. But he was still undeniably cute.

"Thanks for sticking around," he said, in that slow, soft drawl. "Without you, we couldn't have finished tonight."

I moved toward the van, not sure how to reply. "So, who was sexting?" I asked, in an attempt to be funny and, more important, to keep him from hitting on me. Which I somehow knew was the goal behind all of this friendly chit chat.

The problem was that I didn't exactly mind being hit on by him, but if I took one step away from Jeremy, I would take another. And pretty soon, I would settle for the guy who was close, not the one I really wanted.

He laughed. "Everyone's sexting. Except you and me, that is."

I didn't even want to think about that one. "Well," I began, trying to figure out how beat it out of there. "At least we got the paper put to bed." It was a Ms. Snider term, and I regretted it the moment it was out of my mouth.

"You're funny, Logan." He was not getting my message, and it was my fault.

"I didn't mean to say that," I told him, "and for your information, I've never sexted anyone in my life."

"I never thought you did." He smiled, and his dimples deepened. "What I really wanted to ask you about is what happened with Bodmer last week."

At last, a way out of this conversation. "You know about that?"

"Everyone does. Dina's not exactly silent about anything, especially anything having to do with you or your friends."

"That's her problem, and it's all right now. Bodmer returned my phone last Thursday."

"Good." He paused, and I could see that there was still something on his mind.

"What, Sol?"

"I've never seen you text in class," he said.

"You're right. I do sometimes, but never in her class. That day was an exception. It really was."

"A guy, right? That's what I heard it was about."

Why not tell the truth? Soon it would be too dark to see Sol's face. Too dark to be embarrassed by the pity there.

"Right. A guy. He's living in Ireland now. Our time zones are kind of messed up, and we keep missing each other. That's all. I should have known better than to try it in front of Bodmer."

"Same thing happened to me," he said.

"Bodmer caught you texting?"

"Not that. The girl I was seeing in Texas? Suzanne?" He said it like a question, and I knew that I needed to get out of there right now.

"It's not like that with Jeremy and me. We're going to be okay."

"Maybe, maybe not. After my family moved out here, I kept trying to contact her, and she never got back to me. She just stopped. Finally, I called her at home, and her little sister told me it was over. Her twelve-year-old sister. Suzanne couldn't even tell me herself that she was seeing some other guy."

"Oh, geez." I didn't know what else to say.

"It's okay now. All that's left is the anger. The worst part was not knowing what was going on. It was all that wondering and worrying."

"I'm going to keep trying with Jeremy."

"How long did you date him?" he asked.

I tried to ignore his use of the past tense. "We haven't been seeing each other that long, but when it's the right person, you know."

"That's what I thought, and we were together two years. Hey, it's getting cold out here. Would you like to go somewhere and get some coffee?"

"I can't," I said. "I need to spend some time studying the ephemeris."

"We wouldn't have to stay late, just hang out and talk about stuff."

Like our failed romances. The Cancer only wanted to spend time with me so that we could exchange broken-heart stories over lattes.

"Sol," I said. "This isn't a good idea."

"Why not? Are you still hoping to hear from that guy?"

Of course I was.

"I'm just trying really hard to figure out what's coming down the night of the launch party," I said. "I . . ."

At that moment, my phone dinged. A text from a number I didn't know.

"Good thing Bodmer's not here," he said.

"You're right about that." I glanced down at the message.

need to ask u about capricorn guys

call me

now

AW

AW? I didn't know any AW, only . . .

. . . It couldn't be Arianna Woods, could it?

"Who is it?" Sol asked. "The guy from Ireland?"

"No," I said. "You won't believe this, but I think it's Arianna Woods."

"When did you two get so friendly?"

"We're far from friends," I said. "I don't know what she wants."

"Well then, I guess you'd better get back to her." His voice was pleasant enough, but his expression was shut down, maybe angry. For a moment, I wondered if he was confusing me with the girl in Texas who had dumped him, and I was glad I hadn't given in and agreed to coffee.

"Yeah," I said. "I probably should."

"Go for it. See you tomorrow."

I needed Arianna on my side. And now she wanted me to contact her. As Sol walked away from me, his broad shoulders hunched forward, I did just that.

I answered:

serious

caps are serious

can act cold

After my text, Arianna called me, sobbing.

"I need to talk to you," she said. "Get over here right now, will you?"

"I can't," I told her. "I'm back in Terra Bella Beach. Where are you?"

"San Fran, of course. He was supposed to meet me here after the cover shoot. But he's a liar. I can never count on anything he says."

"Who?" I asked.

"Josh Mellick." She began sobbing again. "For the past hour, I've been reading about our signs online, but I can't figure out what it all means. Get here as soon as you can. I've got to know what to do about him."

I wanted to ask where her friends were, but then maybe she didn't have any. At least she was giving me a chance to make up for outing her YUTalk page.

"Okay," I told her, and knew what I had to do. "I can't be there tonight, but I can meet you tomorrow."

"I need someone now," she sobbed. "I need someone to talk to. I really don't want to be alone."

As if there weren't dozens of people she could call. "It will take a few hours. Are you sure . . . ?"

"Please." Her voice was thin, high-pitched and absolutely pathetic.

"Okay," I said. "Just tell me where I need to go."

CRUSHES: HOW TO GET A GEMINI
By Logan McRae

Getting a Gemini guy to notice you is easy. Getting the Gemini to invest in more than a passing interest is a little more difficult.

They live for communication and the exchange of information, and they frequently change their mind. He might ask you out for coffee and decide it would be more fun to stop for a pizza. If you have to stick to a rigid schedule, the Twin will probably decide to just drop you at home.

Here are three ways to get him interested:

• **Talk.** *There's little that impresses him more than a girl who can hold her own in conversation, especially if you can teach him something. Memorize some little-known fact about psychology, language, or what they put in strawberry ice cream, and watch those information junkie Gem eyes light up.*

• **Have opinions.** *The Twin doesn't mind debate and doesn't mind conceding to an informed and articulate girl. This is one guy who will never tell you to shut up.*

• **Welcome the war stories.** *Most Gems have a bunch of broken-heart stories. Feign interest. Even encourage him to talk about former loves. If he asks about yours (and he will), open up.*

What to say when he asks you out: *"That's a great idea. So what are you doing right now?"*

12

WHEN IT COMES TO LOVE, THE GEMINI WOMAN AND THE GEMINI MAN ARE WORLDS APART. SHE'S FALLING IN LOVE WITH EVERYONE, AND BELIEVING THAT EVERY LOVE WILL BE THE FOREVER ONE. HE'S FALLING IN LUST WITH EVERYONE AND SPEAKING OF LOVE AS IF IT IS HIS NATIVE LANGUAGE. THE ONLY WAY TO TRUST GEMINI LOVE IS TO GIVE IT TIME. MUCH TIME. BUT THAT SEEMS TO BE SOMETHING TOO MANY GEMINIS, OF BOTH SEXES, LACK.

—Fearless Astrology

*S*o, there I was, against my better judgment, alone in the dreaded paint van, rattling, squeaking, and without a heater. Yes, I was cold, in the middle of the night, on my way to an A-list hotel in San Francisco, to meet up with the world's biggest pop star.

I wasn't certain if I would make it. The weather was out of a horror film, and the blinding wind and rain would have blown any decent vehicle off the road. The old Chevy van's only positive quality was its weight, thanks to my dad's a/c compressor in the back.

If the van had a sign, it had to be Earth. Sturdy, predictable Taurus, serious, meticulous Virgo, or solemn, hardworking Capricorn. Thinking about my *van's* sign, as a new wave of wind and water hit, made me laugh at myself and this crazy journey I had chosen to take.

As I wove around the curves and over the hills, I listened to the AM radio until the music fizzed in and out and finally disappeared altogether. Then I tried to remember everything I had read about Arianna and *Mellick*, the band that had launched her career.

Cory Scott, the hot and talented guitarist/songwriter, had a thing with her before she began dating Josh Mellick. That triangle was rumored to be the reason she had gone out on her own after the group's first and last big hit. Arianna had shot to the top, leaving Cory and Josh far behind.

Finally, the multitiered lights of the Golden Gate flashed in front of me. All I had to do was find the hotel, and I had printed out directions before I left. No turning back now.

Arianna met me at the door of her suite. She was barefoot and wore a short white dress embroidered with multicolored designs. Even before I entered the room, I could smell the alcohol on her breath.

"Tequila shots," she said, as if acknowledging my not-so-brilliant observation. "Want one?"

"I've been driving for three hours," I told her. "I could use some coffee."

"We'll call room service, but we need to use your name." She walked back into the suite and motioned for me to follow. "It won't be a problem since I used it to register."

I stopped in the doorway. "You used my name? To register for this room?"

"Dude, get over yourself, will you? Last time I used the limo driver's. No one pays any attention to me when I come in wearing a baseball cap and pretend to be someone normal. Hurry up and close the door, will you? It's getting cold in here."

I had driven through the wind and rain to learn more about her astrology chart, and to help her if I could. Now that I realized she was registered under my name, I felt a little weird. If something happened to me here, there would be no connection to her.

"I said close the door."

"I'm not so sure I should," I told her.

"I could have gotten you fired, you know that?" She gave me that look again, but the navy eyes were less hostile. "I still could."

"Why would you do that?"

She sighed, and I realized that she was close to tears. "I don't want to. I'm just saying that I could. Okay?"

"Okay. I also know that you could go to any number of astrologers to the stars for what you want."

"And maybe end up in the tabloids tomorrow. It's happened before." She sat down on the sofa and curled her legs under the dress. On the large screen, an image of her DVD, *Paradox*, played with no sound. "I know I was shitty to you, but you deserved it. I'm willing to give you a second chance."

"I didn't come here because I wanted a second chance, Arianna. I came because you sounded pretty scary on the phone. And because I wanted to help."

"I always get like this when he treats me like crap," she said. "We can't stay together, and we can't stay apart. Just tell me if a Gemini stands a chance with a Capricorn, okay?"

She reached for that tequila bottle again and splashed some into a water glass that was already stuffed to the top with ice.

"Capricorn and Gemini can be really fine together," I said. "A Cardinal versus a Mutable sign. He's take-charge, and you're flexible. Capricorn wants to lead, and Gemini can't be controlled. But both signs share a wonderful gift for wit, and it could definitely work."

She put down her glass on a dark wood table. "Then why isn't it working? Why do we always fight?"

"Maybe this?" I picked up her glass, rattled the ice cubes, and set it down on the table again. "A serious Capricorn is not going to like all of this booze you've got, Arianna."

"I don't drink that much," she said. "In spite of that tabloid trash you've heard. I just do it because I get bored. And because he treats me so bad."

"How's that?"

"He blames me for leaving the band. So does Cory. But I had to. It was the only way I could go after everything I have now."

"Didn't you date Cory before Josh?"

"Dude, for like seconds."

I couldn't help thinking of Gemini Chili. To these Mutable Air signs, forever was a feeling, and not one that lasted all that long.

"Cory was always my favorite," I said. "Of the guys, I mean."

"He had the magic, all right, but it was Josh who made me feel safe." She wiped her eyes. "How did I lose him? How do I get him back? Can you really help me?"

"I don't know, but I can try," I said. "And, by the way, when it comes to love, most Gemini girls are just looking for a hero."

"You mean a daddy, don't you? My dad started a second family a year after he left my mom for the biggest bimbo on the planet. I hate him."

"No you don't." I thought of my own parents. My mom was out there trying to be the golf queen, resenting the hell out of the fact that she'd been slowed down by having to raise a child. Me. My dad was trying to work hard at the ad agency. Slowed down by having to take care of me since my mom bailed. "You have to forgive your parents. We all do."

"I know you're right, but I am so angry. All I want is Josh. If it can work out with him, the rest won't matter."

"Give me his birth information, and I'll do a compatibility chart," I said. "I can't do it tonight, because I have to drive back home so I can get to school tomorrow. But I'll get on it as soon as I can."

"I need it right away," she told me. "It's my only hope."
To have her Rising sign and really dig into her chart would give me the rest of the information I needed, for the column, yes, but also for whatever might be coming down the night of the *CRUSH* launch party. I'd be helping her in more ways than one, regardless of what happened with Josh and her.

"I'll start on it right away."

"You really do know this stuff, don't you?" She pushed her thick hair out of her eyes. "Stacy said you're trying out for a column."

"Yeah, I am." I didn't know how much I was supposed to say, but I was only confirming what Stacy had already told her.

"What do you have to do to get the gig?"

"Just make some predictions about the launch party. I've been forecasting where the stars will be that night, and it could be, well, explosive."

"I hope not," she said, and it was all I could do to keep from telling her that the explosive stuff was in her Gemini/Aries chart. "Stacy's really stressing, though. She told me about the elevator getting stuck."

"More than stuck," I said. "Somebody turned off the power and cut the phone cord."

"Really? You don't think someone is trying to hurt you, do you?"

"Of course not, but Alex Keen was in the elevator too, and a lot of people knew he'd be there."

She began to fidget with her glass. "Who'd want to harm him?"

"I'm not sure," I told her. "My astrological sources are old, and sometimes, the language changes. I just need to do a lot more research on Alex. Do you know him?"

"No, and I don't care about what happens to him." She stood up and crossed her arms over her chest. "All that matters to me is keeping Josh. Call as soon as you have the chart, okay? I've got stuff to do now."

After demanding that I drive three hours?

I stood up as well. "Are you sure you want me to leave?" I asked.

"Sorry." She flashed me a nervous smile. "Thanks for coming. I have another appointment in a few minutes. Drive safely, okay?"

She closed the door behind me. Maybe just a little too fast.

So, all of a sudden, Arianna had an "appointment," after insisting hours ago that she had no one to talk to? Henry Jaffa told me that if you pay attention, you can smell a lie. I was smelling one now.

Might as well try to follow her, since I was here anyway. I went over to the alcove in the hall across and down from her room. If anyone noticed me with my book, they'd think I was studying and not getting ready to stalk a star.

Minutes passed—five, ten, fifteen—and still no Arianna. Just as I was deciding that this was crazy and I really should drive home, the door to her room opened a crack. I put the book up to my face and peered around it. Any moment now, she would step outside. But she didn't. Why was she hesitating?

A guy dressed in white hurried past me, mumbling something on a cell phone. Although the chef outfit hid most of his body, nothing concealed those blond curls of his. The door to Arianna's suite opened slowly, cautiously. Alex Keen rushed inside.

CRUSHES: HOW TO CAPTIVATE A CANCER
By Logan McRae

The Crab is going to be less interested in what you're like on the outside and more interested in how much you understand him. If you have an insensitive bone in your body, believe me, he can tell it a mile away.

Cancers are also protective of their possessions, and if you spill soda in his car or accidentally delete a special photo from his cell phone, you probably won't get much farther into his life. Here are three ways you can captivate him.

• **Nurture.** *If he has a cold, bring him chicken soup. If you know he has to come in early to study, drop by with his favorite coffee drink, then leave before he's distracted by anything other than your thoughtfulness.*

• **Show interest.** *Ask casual questions about his parents and sibs. Cancers are always tied to their families, some in a good way; some not. Showing that you're a good listener will score big points.*

• **Be romantic.** *A funny card that goes almost over the line, but not quite. A text about an assignment with a compliment at the end. Romantic gestures will get that Crab out of his shell.*

What to say when he asks you out: *"I thought you'd never call!"*

13

THOSE WITH THE SAME ELEMENTS (FIRE, EARTH, AIR, OR WATER) ARE SAID TO BE TRINED (CONNECTED) AND USUALLY RELATE WELL AND OFTEN INSTANTLY TO EACH OTHER. BUT YOUR CLOSE FRIENDS DO NOT HAVE TO BE TRINED. A PASSIONATE FIRE CAN APPRECIATE THE DETERMINATION OF AN EARTH SIGN, THE COMMUNICATION SKILLS OF AN AIR SIGN, AND THE EMOTIONS OF A WATER SIGN.

—*Fearless Astrology*

Had I really seen what I thought I had last night? Were Alex and Arianna together? Poor Chili. No way could I begin to discuss it with her. Arianna and I were trined because she the Gemini, and I the Aquarius, were both Air signs. And although I did feel sorry for her, I couldn't trust her now that I knew she lied about knowing Alex.

It was the middle of the night by the time I got home. I managed to sneak in without waking my dad and was so exhausted that I didn't know how I would wake up in time for class. I did it, though. When Chili and Paige picked me up that morning, they were both still excited about our trip.

"I got a text from Alex," Chili said. "I'm going to bring him some of my mom's recipes when we drive you up on Friday. Can you believe this is happening?"

I could believe it, all right, and I was already blaming myself. "What does Stella say?" I asked.

"Just the usual Armenian mom stuff. That even though my dad's older than she is, there's no way she would allow me to date a twenty-one-year-old guy, no matter how famous he is. That kind of stuff."

"It sounds pretty sensible to me," I said.

"Since when are you sensible?" Both she and Paige laughed, but I couldn't.

"What happened with that elevator was pretty scary. A lot of people knew that Alex would be in it."

"You don't think it was an accident?" Chili asked.

"I'm not sure. I'm just saying . . ."

"Well if anyone messed with the elevator, it was Francis, the head chef. Can you believe that old guy?"

"He was probably just upset because he had to turn over his kitchen to a celebrity chef who hasn't paid his dues," I said.

She stared straight ahead as if trying to make eye contact with the road. "You don't sound very happy for me, Logan."

"I'm just worried, that's all."

"We were worried about Jeremy," Paige piped up from the back. "But we supported you, even though we knew the relationship didn't have much of a chance." The words came out so easily, as if Jeremy and I were already over and done.

My eyes burned. "You're right, Paige," I said. "All this magazine stuff is making me crazy. I do think something is going to happen at the Halloween launch party, and Alex might be involved."

"How can you be so sure?" Chili asked.

I couldn't tell her that I had seen him go into Arianna's hotel room right after I left. At least not now when Chili was so determined that he was guy of her dreams. "I told you. Because of what happened on the elevator."

"Can't you check his chart?"

"I'm going to, but I can't find the year he was born."

"I told you he's twenty-one." Chili turned to me looking like her old mischievous self. "I can find out everything else for you when we go there Friday."

"How are you going to get out of school?" I asked.

"Head cold," Chili said, and faked a cough.

"Cramps," Paige whined.

I had to smile. They had already figured it out. "On a Friday?" I asked. "All three of us? That's pretty suspicious."

"What are they going to do?" Chili said, "Demand that we take a lie detector test? I've got to go there because I have a plan. I'm going to be so cute, hot, and interested in everything that he invites me to be his date for the launch party. What do you think?"

What did I think? That she was absolutely out of her mind. "If anyone can do it, you will."

"And I'm designing their costumes," Paige said. "Chili will be Catwoman, and Alex will be Batman."

"And you," Chili said, "are going to be Sherlock Holmes. But don't worry. It's a very sexy design, and super short to show off your great legs. I saw Paige's sketches."

Sherlock Holmes? Not a famous writer. Still, I kind of liked it. "What are you going to be, Paige?" I asked.

She shrugged. "I don't know, but it's got to be good to impress the Platinum Dragon. If I could only grow a body like Chili's."

"You don't need a body like anyone's," I said. "You look great, and you have the talent. But tell me, why am I only now hearing about these costumes you two have been planning for us?"

"Well." Chili glanced back at Paige. "We weren't sure how you would react to my mission of getting Alex to take me to the party. Come on, Logan, he is so fabulous. Please be happy for me."

As we pulled into the parking lot, I remembered how I felt when Jeremy had kissed me for the first time. How I felt that last day he said he loved me. Sure, the odds were against us, but no one could have told me that at the time.

I climbed out of the car, hugged her, and said, "I am happy for you. And, just for the record, Alex doesn't stand a chance against a hot Gemini."

"Hi, Chili. Hi Paige. Hiiii, Logan." Dina came toward us in the parking lot, still wearing her new flat hairstyle.

"Hi," I said, just so she wouldn't start telling kids I was snotty.

"So is it true?" she asked. "About the party?"

I exchanged looks with Chili and Paige. "What party?"

"The costume party for *CRUSH*," she said, with a smirk. "Is it true that you girls are going?"

I shrugged. "Where'd you hear that?"

"Chili told Sol in journalism."

"All I said . . ." Her face turned pink.

". . . Is that Logan is getting you and Paige into the party." Dina beamed at me. "So, what I'm wondering is will this take place before or after the *CRUSH* model is announced?"

"Halloween," I mumbled, feeling my own face flush.

"Before or after?" She cocked her head, ready to pounce on whatever I said next.

"I'm not sure. Before, I think."

"That's what I thought. See you later." She left the parking lot, almost running, her A-line top hiking up above her new skinny jeans.

NOTES TO SELF

That talkative Gemini has gotten me in trouble. Now Kat is going to claim that we are influencing Graciela to select Chili as our school's model. Chili tried to explain that she was just so excited that she had to tell someone. And that someone happened to be the school newspaper editor. Now everyone is going to hate me. I need to talk to someone I can trust, someone reliable, like a Taurus. Maybe it's time I actually called Jeremy. I take out my cell and look at the photo I took of him on the beach before he left. That thick, dark hair. Those Taurus eyes. I can still see the love in them. He didn't fake that. He couldn't have.

WHAT KIND OF FRIEND ARE YOU?

Aries: *Exciting*
Taurus: *Dependable*
Gemini: *Fun*
Cancer: *Supportive*
Leo: *Outgoing*
Virgo: *Organized*
Libra: *Tolerant*
Scorpio: *Loyal*
Sagittarius: *Optimistic*
Capricorn: *Practical*
Aquarius: *Honest*
Pisces: *Creative*

14

TRUST THE STARS. THEY ARE NEVER WRONG. SOME WHO
CLAIM TO UNDERSTAND THEM ARE. SOME WHO HOPE TO
UNDERSTAND THEM ARE. BUT NEVER THE STARS.

—*Fearless Astrology*

odmer waved at me in the hall. She wore one of her many pairs of black pants—flared ones this time—with a pleated burgundy top and the usual accompanying scarf. Today that scarf was purple and green.

"Cool about the *CRUSH* party, Logan. I'm proud of you. Get Alex Keen's autograph for me, will you? I have all of his cookware."

So the confiscated cell phone incident was behind us, and an Alex Keen autograph opportunity lay ahead. Good, except that Bodmer was speaking in her raspy, animated chemistry-teacher voice, which meant that what she had just said could probably be heard all the way to Santa Barbara.

"The launch party thing is supposed to be confidential," I told her.

"Why wouldn't you want to share such wonderful news?" She reached up into her streaked tangle of curls, pulled out a pair of sunglasses, but didn't put them on.

"Because not everyone thinks it's wonderful."

"What do you care? If you were worried about spite, jealousy, and cruel high school gossip, you wouldn't be where you are, would you?" She started to put on the glasses. "Think it over. I'll see you in class."

"Wait," I said. "I need to ask you something."

"What is it? Are you okay? You're not letting all of this gossip get to you, are you?"

"I'm fine. It doesn't have anything to do with that." I hated the way my voice broke.

"What then?"

"I was just wondering when your birthday is."

She laughed. "I'm a Taurus. That's what you really want to know, isn't it? Fixed Earth saved by a Leo Moon."

"So that's where you get the hair," I blurted. "I'm sorry. I didn't mean . . ."

"Of course you did," she said. "I believe in science, including the sciences we don't yet fully understand. Other teachers around here don't, so you might want to keep a low profile about all of that."

"I have," I said, and thought about Ms. Snider and her threat to end my internship if I didn't give up astrology.

"Maybe not quite low enough."

I didn't like the way she said it. "What do you mean?"

"You've had some good luck in the last year. You're having some good luck right now. All it takes is one jealous person to suggest that it's more than luck."

"What?" I asked. "That I'm a demon or something?"

She gave me that steady yet concerned look again. "All I'm saying is be careful about how much you talk about astrology, Logan. Not everyone understands that it's just science. Not evil."

"Evil? Now, that's crazy."

"Some thought electricity was evil. A light goes on, and insecure people get scared." She patted my shoulder. "You're on a roll right now. Just protect yourself, okay?"

"I'll try," I said.

"And Logan." She grinned. "I think you're awesome."

"Thanks." I wanted to say I thought she was the awesome one, but I was too upset by what she had told me.

I hadn't gotten far, when Chili appeared from around the building. This morning, she had looked happy and in love in her blue-leopard print top and skinny jeans. Now she looked confused, maybe even scared.

She ran up to me and motioned me off to the side.

"What's wrong?" I asked.

"It's Kat." She looked around and then lowered her voice. "That little bitch is telling everyone that you're not normal. That you are some kind of . . ."

". . . Witch?" I asked.

"How'd you know?"

"Bodmer." I felt sick. "The rumor is already viral."

"She's saying that's how you got the internship, how you got us invited to the *CRUSH* party. She says you're going to use it to get me picked for the magazine swimsuit spread."

"As if your face and body have nothing to do with it." I was starting to get angry and remembered Bodmer's advice. "If they're so freaking stupid that they think astrology is witchcraft, that's their problem."

"Except," she said, "Somehow Kat found out about what happened in Monterey."

"So what? I solved a very old mystery."

"And some people got in trouble. Kat's telling kids that anyone who crosses you ends up in trouble."

"Because of Monterey?"

"Not just that."

Oh, that's right. What had happened at the end of my sophomore year, when I had first discovered *Fearless Astrology* and figured out a solution to a totally different mystery. That's what she was talking about.

"So Kat claims it's witchcraft and not astrology that has helped me solve two mysteries? And she's trying to make kids think I might use it on them?"

"You don't get it," Chili said. "Kat thinks astrology is witchcraft. She thinks you're using it for your own gain, and that you're willing to use it on anyone to get what you want."

"Thanks, Chili," I told her. "I have more important issues to worry about than what Kat or anyone else at this school thinks about me. And so do you."

"You're right about that." The Gemini multitasking mind clicked into hot-guy gear. "Alex, for instance. I got another text from him last night. Eeee!"

I bit back the impulse to say, *Be careful*. Tried to shut off the film in my mind of him sneaking into Arianna's suite.

We hugged each other, went our separate directions, and I was left with how I really felt about this newest development. So astrology was now witchcraft according the gospel of Kat? I had been ridiculed, even hated, at this school before.

Other than a few Goth kids, no one looked or spoke to me. Not that they obviously avoided me. They just made it a point to be noticing someone else or heading another direction when they realized that I was anywhere near them. It didn't hurt me the way it had the first time, and it probably wouldn't have hurt at all if I knew that I still had Jeremy.

That night, my dad came home earlier than usual from the ad agency. I was at the kitchen counter with my laptop, trying to read about the sign of Sagittarius. It was the best I could do. Trying to do an Internet search for Alex Keen's year of birth hadn't turned up a thing.

"Hi, sweetheart." He entered the room with less certainty now. Before he and my mom separated, he was the force and the energy in this house. "Anything you need?"

A family would be nice. Of course, I didn't tell him that. "I'm okay, Dad."

"Have you eaten?"

"Some leftover pilaf and shish kebab."

"Want one of my instant fabulous pizzas?"

"I'm okay. I really am."

Without food to prepare, he looked a little lost. I realized that cooking for me was his preferred method of communication.

"Could you use some extra money?"

Now that was extremely out-of-character for his Virgo self, which he would define as simply thrifty, and I might call cheap.

"I'm fine. Thanks."

"Well, sweetheart, as an intern at *CRUSH*, you probably should be updating your wardrobe, shouldn't you?" So this wasn't about Virgo tightwad parting with money. It was about my internship.

"I'm doing all right at the magazine. And my editor likes the way I dress."

"I'm really proud of you. Everything you've accomplished, you've done it on your own. You know that don't you? Astrology only helped, but you were the one who made it happen."

"Thanks," I said. "Not everyone at school is seeing it that way at the moment."

"Jillian told me." *The art teacher*. What was he doing talking to Jillian Berry—Cherry Berry, as we called her—when he and Mom had barely split?

"Did she tell you that they're calling me a witch?"

His pained expression gave me a glimpse of how he would look when he was old. "Anyone who equates astrology with witchcraft is uninformed. You can't worry about them."

"Not even when they're the whole school?"

"They aren't the whole school, Logan. It just feels that way right now. You're going to be fine. And if you have to lay off of the astrology for awhile, do it."

"I can't lay off, Dad. I haven't told you this, but I'm trying out to write an astro column for *CRUSH*. Henry Jaffa supports me all the way."

"Henry Jaffa? He's pretty cool, all right. I can see how you would want to please him." He sat down next to me at the counter. "I know you've got a lot of questions right now. Do you think perhaps before we discuss anything else, that maybe we need to talk about what's happening with Mom and me?"

"No, I'm fine. Just fine. And I'm exhausted, Dad. I need to go to bed now. Let's talk in the morning, okay?"

Then, before I could burst into tears, I jumped off of the stool and rushed down the hall and inside my room.

I sat on my bed, so scared that I could barely move. I was afraid to reach out to Jeremy once more, but I had to. It couldn't be over until I knew what was going on with him. No way could I move forward until I knew the truth about us. I stared down at the phone in my hand and pressed the key to connect me to him. Was I really doing this? Yes, I was. And it felt so good and so terrible.

"You've reached Jeremy's phone. He's not here right now. Leave your message, please."

I almost dropped the telephone. The soft, sexy voice on the recording was female, and not Irish at all. The inflection was closer to Boston than Dublin. What could that possibly mean? How could I possibly respond?

"I love you, Jeremy," I said into the phone, as if I could

drown out her voice by doing so. "Please call me when you get this message. I need to talk to you."

CRUSHES: HOW TO LAND A LEO
By Logan McRae

This Sun-ruled guy is used to center stage. Whether he is a quiet Leo or the in-your-face entertainer Lion, he loves—and expects—attention. Shower him with it, and he'll be happy to share the spotlight with you.

Don't embarrass him in public, though, and don't make a joke at his expense. Leo expects his audience, including you, to be an admiring one.

Three ways to get him to admire you:

• **Be entertained.** *Encourage his antics. Laugh at his jokes. He'll be pleased that you're pleased—and that you have such good taste.*

• **Dress the part.** *He wants a date who can share the spotlight with him. Cute, attention-getting clothes will help him picture you in that role.*

• **Be friendly.** *Chat up his friends (but don't flirt). Be likeable and fun-loving.*

What to say when he asks you out: *"I'm so glad you called. I was just thinking about you."*

15

BE READY FOR CHANGES IN YOUR LIFE. THE GOOD
ALONG WITH THE NOT-SO GOOD. FOR FIRE SIGNS
(ARIES, LEO, SAGITTARIUS), CHANGE COMES WITH
THE TERRITORY, A WAY OF LIFE. FOR EARTH SIGNS
(TAURUS, VIRGO, CAPRICORN), CHANGE IS OFTEN OFF
LIMITS. YET AIR SIGNS (GEMINI, LIBRA, AQUARIUS)
OFTEN CRAVE CHANGE LIKE, WELL, AIR. AND WATER
SIGNS (CANCER, SCORPIO, PISCES) FREQUENTLY
REFUSE TO AND FORGET HOW TO CHANGE, UNTIL THEY
FINALLY WAKEN TO THE REALITY OF THEIR SITUATION.

—*Fearless Astrology*

quarius is Fixed Air, which means we aren't as adaptable to change unless we initiate it. I sure wasn't liking the changes in my life. Why had Jeremy changed the message on his phone? And who was that girl? I could only hope he would call back soon.

I was grateful for a chance to escape that Friday to San Francisco. Chili and Paige had their excuses for missing that day. Head cold for Chili, and cramps for Paige. We arrived in the city and broke through the fog the same time the sun did.

We were supposed to be at the hotel early, and, thanks to Chili we were. The wind was sharp and damp, but fall was actually summer in the city, and the weather wouldn't stay cold for long. I was glad that I'd worn my gray knit beanie, which would at least keep the back part of my hair from frizzing. Paige had no worries in that department. Her pale hair was pulled up into a messy bun the wind only enhanced. She carried a notebook that she had told us contained sketches for Stacy's Queen of Hearts costume. Her goal in her jeans, white shirt, and herringbone heels, clearly was to look older, and she was pulling it off.

Chili's goal was, although different, just as obvious. The low-cut top, layered over a tank, clung to her curvy frame and killer glutes. Tiny gold beads glittered in the black mesh sweater that flowed around her, and the simple white pants made her seem both proper and sexy.

"If you two looked any better," I said, "they would fire Arianna, put you on the cover of the magazine, and save a ton of money."

Chili laughed. "Tell me the truth. Do I look casual enough?"

"That's not exactly the word I was thinking of," I said. "Nothing about your butt in white pants is even remotely casual. I think you'll get the response you want from a certain chef, though."

"That's the plan. Paige designs Stacy's costume. I get Alex to take me to the party. You get the astro column. Great goals, aren't they?"

My lip quivered. Couldn't help it. I wanted so much more than the column. I wanted Jeremy. How sick was that, when he had another girl's voice on his voice mail now?

Paige stepped between Chili and me on the sidewalk. "It's okay, Logan. Maybe Jeremy is traveling with his dad or something. You said he was going to do that."

"Sure. Maybe." This wasn't the time to explain to them about the voice on his phone.

The hotel waited ahead. This time we took the real elevator. Weird, but I still felt nervous. Chili edged beside me, and I knew that she was remembering last Friday in the service elevator as well.

As we got off, Alex Keen pushed his way inside, all full of himself, blond curls perfectly styled to appear anything but.

"Alex," Chili said. "What's going on?"

"My chef's kit. My freaking knives." That was his hello. The slam-shut sound of the elevator door was his good bye.

"He didn't even look at me." Chili said. "What did I do wrong?"

"Nothing," I told her. "He'll be back once he finds his stuff.

Don't worry. Knives to people in his business are like underwear to us."

That made her smile. "I'm not exactly concerned about underwear, if you know what I mean."

I glanced down at the white pants, that smooth curve from waist to leg.

"Chili, you didn't go commando for this."

"Well, actually, I . . ."

"Hey, Logan."

For a moment, I thought of Dina's insane greetings at school. Wrong scenario. I turned in the direction of the husky cheerleader voice.

There, emerging from a huddle of hotel staffers, stood Arianna, hair cascading over her shoulders. She wore only a spray-on tan and two strips of multicolored fabrics, one on top, one on bottom. I realized that they matched her hair, and that every inch of her killer flesh must have been waxed. That was the only way she could show that much of herself.

"Hi," I managed.

"Just finished the second photo shoot." Once she made sure everyone in the room had checked her out, she slipped into a sea-green ruana that covered most of her top and drifted around the rest of her.

"You can't believe what's going on here this morning," she said. "Someone stole Alex Keen's knives. He's doing his usual nonstop rant."

"So we gathered. We passed him on the elevator."

Before I could say anything else, I realized that she was

not alone. Behind her, stood Cory Scott. Make that towered. His blue-black hair was longer, his jaw even stronger than what I remembered from *Mellick*. And he was beyond my wildest dream cute.

"Cory," she said, "This is Logan, the astrology chick I was telling you about."

"Ari told me that you drove all the way up here to help her out," he said. "I guess I'm your reward."

Now I felt totally clueless, the punchline of the joke. I wasn't sure if I could speak.

"I'm sorry. I . . ."

"Dude, stop teasing her." Arianna nudged him. "Can't you see she's nervous? You'll get used to him, Logan. When you told me how much you liked him, I thought you might want to interview him for your college newspaper."

College newspaper. I didn't know what to do. He thought I was a college student. How had Arianna screwed that up? It was too late to try to explain, and I wasn't going to tell him otherwise. I just needed to get away from him and this ridiculous situation.

"Works for me." Cory grinned again. "Ari needed you that night. She deserved way more than she was hoping for from someone else."

"Who?" The moment I spoke the word I knew that I shouldn't have. I also reminded myself that Cory had been Arianna's boyfriend before she'd gotten together with Josh.

"Forget about that," he said. "All I know is that I'm a Scorpio. Too secretive and sexy. Right?"

"Cool," I muttered, and my cheeks burned. "You already know about astrology?"

"Just enough to understand a few things."

"Well, you're right. Scorpio is a Water sign. Lots of deep emotions, moods, and secrecy there. But your Sun sign is just part of it. What's your Moon?"

"I don't know. Can you figure it out?" He moved close to me, invaded my personal space, and didn't seem to care. I wasn't sure if I cared either. "And aren't you going to interview me?"

For a college newspaper that doesn't exist. Uh, not.

"Interview him," Arianna demanded. "Your college friends will love it."

Except I wasn't in college. I was only a junior at Terra High.

Cory hadn't taken his eyes from me. They were nice eyes too, pale blue highlighted by thick, black lashes.

Just then I realized that maybe an article about him in the Terra High paper was just what I needed to restore my credibility. No one would think I was a witch who was out to get them if I interviewed the cutest guy on the planet.

"You're right," I told Arianna. "All of my friends love Cory."

"And what about you?" Those eyes focused on mine. I realized I was living a dream, and I had no idea how to step out of that dream and get back to my real life.

"Me too," I said. "When can I interview you?"

"Right now?"

This guy was too hot, too famous to be looking at me like this. But he was, he was, he was. All I could do was my best.

He took my arm, and chills shot through me. "There's a table over there by the balcony. Want to . . ."

"What the hell have you done with my knives?"

Alex Keen stormed into the room, and immediately took ownership of it.

Francis, the hotel chef, glanced up from the menu he held. "Surely you misplaced them."

"I don't misplace, and I don't lose."

"Interesting. One of the waiters found this inside the smoker." He reached into a cardboard box and took out a cloth-wrapped bundle.

Alex snatched it from him. "Very funny. I didn't leave them there, and you know it."

Francis shrugged. "I have no idea how well you take care of your property. You're lucky they weren't thrown out." Head held high, he turned and left the room.

Alex glared after him. Then slowly, he turned toward us and broke into a Sagittarius smile.

"There you are," he said to Chili in that disarming accent. "Sorry I was delayed. Jealous old chefs are so very boring, aren't they?"

Cory and I exchanged glances, and Chili and Alex went off to bond over the kufta and the yalanchi.

"What's your sign?" Cory asked me. "Libra?"

"Why would you say that?" I could barely hold my pen, but I needed to get down the sound of his voice, the black tee he wore, his tanned arms, those biceps.

"Just a guess. Libras are Air signs, and they're articulate, aren't they?"

"Sometimes," I told him, and tried not to gush. "I'm Air too. Aquarius."

"So my guess wasn't too far off. I used to date an Aquarius. You seem more down-to-earth than she was."

"Aries Rising," I said. "Not sure how down-to-earth that is."

"Fiery." He made it sound like the sexiest word in the world.

"We'll have to find out yours," I said, "as soon as we finish the interview. I really appreciate your doing this, Cory."

"I'm happy to. When Ari asked me, she said you were cute. She just didn't say how cute."

My cheeks were blazing. "Thanks. Um, do you think we could get started now?"

"Whatever you like." He pulled the chair close to mine, and I could smell his subtle citrus scent. "Are you with anyone?"

"I drove up with Chili," I said.

"I meant are you with a guy?" He grinned. "Do you have a boyfriend?"

"Yes." I could hardly get the word out.

"Too bad." He pulled his chair even closer. Our arms were almost touching. "And now tell me what you need to know for this article you're writing."

CRUSHES: HOW TO IMPRESS A VIRGO
By Logan McRae

Beneath his careful planning and orchestrated life, that Virgo guy is as critical of himself as he is of those who don't live up to his standards. But if he's hot, and you're into him, you can use his interest in organization, health, and attention to detail to your sneaky little advantage.

If your own life is a mess, know that you don't stand much of a chance with this guy. He'd only try to change you anyway, and then you'd both go crazy. If you think it might work, here are three ways to give yourself the best chance:

• **Dress immaculately.** *Discover that artifact known as the iron, and use it. Linens and natural fabrics are the best way to impress that Virgo's critical eye.*

• **Ask for advice.** *How did he go about preparing that last project with such perfection? What's the best way to research your current assignment in French? Ask for details. Prepare to spend some time listening to them.*

• **Shine in your own right.** *If you write, paint, sing, or do any fun, artistic thing better than this Earth sign, you'll stand out from the crowd.*

What to say when he asks you out: *"Great. What's your plan, where are we going, and what should I wear?"*

16

LISTEN, AND YOU WILL HEAR WHAT YOU MUST LEARN
IN ANY SITUATION, REGARDLESS OF HOW DIFFICULT IT
MAY SEEM. FIRE SIGNS, DO NOT IGNITE. EARTH SIGNS,
DO NOT INSIST. AIR SIGNS, DO NOT ARGUE. WATER
SIGNS, DO NOT IGNORE. JUST LISTEN.

—*Fearless Astrology*

It really happened. I really did interview Cory Scott,
who was more than a little flirty. Arianna was generous
to introduce me to him like that, and there was no way I
could correct her when she said I wrote for a college newspaper. He had a Virgo Moon, which probably made him even
more self-critical and hardworking than most Scorpios.

I'm wasn't going to kid myself, though. I knew that Cory
could never be interested in me. When he asked me if I

would be at the launch party and said he hoped to see me there, he was probably just trying to give me a thrill. And that's exactly what he did. Still, he was just a fantasy, and with my phone continually silent and the memory of that girl's voice in my head, I could use a little fantasy in my life.

Chili, Paige, and I talked nonstop from San Francisco to Terra Bella Beach. Chili announced that she had succeeded in her attempt to impress Alex. He had invited her to the launch party with him. We spent the rest of the trip discussing important, life-changing subjects such as what we would wear.

Paige had already worked on designs for Catwoman and Batman, even before Alex asked Chili. She took out her sketches and passed them to me in the front seat. My Sherlock Holmes costume was short and edgy, complete with mini trench coat, houndstooth hat, magnifying glass, calabash pipe—and a convenient pocket notebook.

I told her I loved it, and I did. I would need the powers of Sherlock if I was going to figure out how to stop whatever was going to happen the weekend of the party.

I realized that it had been almost a month since I had gotten the internship. That Monday, kids were friendlier but still looking at me weird, as if wondering if I might stop in my tracks and put a hex on them. I started to wait outside the cafeteria for Chili and Paige, and then decided not to be a coward.

Terra High was a small school, and so was the cafeteria. Its walls were washed with a light aqua tint that was supposed to remind us that we were a beach school. The padded backs of our benches were once the same color, but they had faded and cracked over the years. It was only a big long room with lots of people in it, I reminded myself. Nothing to fear.

Still, I hesitated just inside the door.

"Hey." Sol headed toward me, and I was actually glad. His pale blue shirt matched his eyes, and in the sun, he had almost as many highlights as Chili. I wondered if they were natural. I could never tell with guys and always assumed that girls' highlights were not. "How was your weekend?"

It seemed strange to hear the polite southern speech coming from such a California-looking guy.

"Okay, I guess. What's up?"

"Dina," he said. "She's been squawking to Ms. Snider about the *CRUSH* launch party."

"I know." I sighed. "Saying that I cast a spell on the magazine editor so that I could somehow get Chili picked as our school's model."

He laughed. "That's pretty close. I just thought you should know in case Ms. Snider says something to you."

I started to get a nervous feeling. It was the same way I had felt when Snider took my astrology column away from me earlier this year. "Do you think she will?"

"Not based on what just one student says."

"Especially when the student is Dina, Kat's only friend in the whole school." I turned away from the door and walked back on the patio. No way could I go in there right now.

"Chill," he said. "Kat and Dina are only two people. They'd have to turn the whole school against you."

"They did it before. Back me up, Sol."

"You know I will do everything I can." He stared into my eyes with a look that said way too much. "What are you doing after school? Maybe we can figure something out."

"I think I need to talk to Snider," I said, trying to avoid his borderline invitation. "I'm not looking forward to it, but I've got to make her understand that attending the party will not help Chili win."

"She's right over there." He nodded to his left, and there was Snider, all right.

She was talking to Mr. Franklin, the gruff English teacher, who hadn't been so gruff once he had started spending time with her. At least I might catch her in a good mood.

She gave me a friendly but curious look, and I wondered if she suspected what Sol was telling me.

I waved at both of them and started toward her just as Franklin waved back and headed toward his classroom.

"I was just telling Sol about the killer interview I got on Friday," I said, then realized that Sol was right beside me. "With Cory Scott."

Other than a slight raise of her eyebrows, I couldn't read her expression. "Sounds good," she said.

"Sol and I think—I mean, I think—it will help dispel the rumors that Dina and Kat are spreading about me. I'm no witch. I'm just a kid who's into astrology, which, by the way, so is Cory."

Her pale cheeks looked ready to burn off her face, and she glared at Sol. "Have you two been discussing Dina's concerns?"

"No," he began awkwardly, clearly not comfortable with lying. "We just . . ."

"Everyone's been telling me what she said." I did my best to cover for him. "And frankly, I'm fed up. I'm working hard on the internship, and I'm learning more about journalism than I ever have in school."

"It's because of the astrology," Snider said. "I warned you about what could happen."

"It's not witchcraft."

"I know that, but you can't stop people from making assumptions."

"You can," I said. "If you let me run the Cory Scott interview, I'll include a definition and point out that it isn't some kind of evil spell."

"I don't know."

"You also need to let us run an article about the CRUSH judging. If kids know what the judging process is they'll be less likely to believe the rumors that Dina is spreading."

"You have a point there," she said. "Do you know what the judging process is?"

"Sure." Not a lie. Graciela Perez would make the decision. I could find out more on Friday at the magazine.

"Well." She gave me a cool little smile, that for this Capricorn, probably felt like a major display of affection. "I'm glad you discussed this with me, Logan. I've talked to some of the other teachers, and I realize that not everyone shares my opinion about astrology."

Thank you, Bodmer. Thank you, Franklin. I was certain they had stood up for me.

"So you'll let me run the interview with Cory?"

"I'll have to look at it first," she said. "And of course, so will Sol."

"Of course," he said in a voice that tried but so totally failed to sound objective.

NOTES TO SELF

Well, that wasn't so bad. At least now Snider knows where I stand on astrology. Now maybe she'll be more understanding when I tell her I'm trying out for the column for *CRUSH*. But I won't be telling her that just yet. Sol was almost as excited as I was by her reaction. A Texas/California laid-back version of excited, that is. Proud of himself, too. He said he had known he needed to tell me about Dina's complaints. And again he asked me what I was doing after school. I used the tired old homework excuse. And even though I thanked him for his help, I could tell he didn't believe me. First I need to figure out how Graciela Perez plans to judge the model contest. I know I can get that out of Stacy. I have to.

CRUSHES: HOW TO LURE A LIBRA

By Logan McRae

Beauty-loving Libra, like Taurus, is ruled by Venus. This guy is probably smart, and probably also looking for a girl who can hold her own in an intelligent conversation. Although his interests are broad, he frequently talks about himself. Not because he's an ego-freak. He's just still trying to figure out who he is and assumes that you're as interested in that topic as he is.

Here are three ways you can make him want to figure out who you are:

• **Pile on the compliments.** *That doesn't mean you have to lie. There's much to praise about most Libra guys, and those guys never get tired of hearing about it. Tell him you love that new shirt he's wearing. You probably do. Say the paper he wrote for English was soulful and deep. It probably was. Tell him you'd kill for his eyelashes. You probably would.*

• **Talk.** *Especially about relationships. Girls aren't the only ones who like to dwell on every moment of love gone bad, or love, period. That Libra guy—who still can't figure out why anyone would want to leave wonderful him—is all too willing to talk. Be the willing listener and watch his interest grow.*

• **Ignore the wishy-washy Libra gene.** *This isn't a Virgo you're dealing with. Make it clear that you understand that everything isn't a case of black-and-white. Appreciate or at least* *tolerate the gray. Your Libra hunk may vacillate now and then, agonizing over whether to order a grande or a venti. Make it clear that you don't care, and you could make him care.*

What to say when he asks you out: *"Wear that cool shirt you had on Thursday. The one that matches your eyes."*

17

WHEN IT COMES TO MANIPULATION, EVEN THE
STRONGEST SIGN IS VULNERABLE. FIRE SIGNS (ARIES,
LEO, SAGITTARIUS) CAN BE MANIPULATED BY ACTION. IF
YOU WANT A FIRE SIGN'S INTEREST, GET BUSY DOING
SOMETHING. AIR SIGNS (GEMINI, LIBRA, AQUARIUS)
CAN BE MANIPULATED BY LANGUAGE. WORDS, ESPE-
CIALLY PRETTY ONES, INTRIGUE THEM. EARTH SIGNS
(TAURUS, VIRGO, CAPRICORN) CAN BE MANIPULATED BY
ACHIEVEMENT. APPEAR SUCCESSFUL (WEALTHY DOESN'T
HURT EITHER), AND YOU'LL GAIN THEIR INTEREST.
WATER SIGNS (CANCER, SCORPIO, PISCES) CAN BE
MANIPULATED BY SECURITY. TO WIN ONE, APPEAR
STABLE AND STRONG, AND THE ANSWER TO A DREAM.

—Fearless Astrology

*D*riving to San Francisco in a rickety paint van was a far different experience than heading up there with my friends. A louder and bumpier experience, but also, a quieter one, because I could hear only myself. Only the questions and answers in my own mind. At least it wasn't raining today, and the winds had slowed down.

Chili and Paige couldn't risk taking off the second Friday in a row, and maybe that was just as well. Chili and Alex were texting and e-mailing all of the time. I still hadn't told her about seeing him go into Arianna's suite that night. I knew that I would have to sooner or later, but this wasn't the time.

After witnessing the many true loves of Jessica Chili Chiliderian from the first grade on, I guessed that this forever passion probably wouldn't make it past the magazine's launch party, Armenian appetizers or not.

That sounded like a cold, analytical Aquarian evaluation, but it really was not. I knew my friend. Chili wouldn't nurse a broken heart a moment longer than it took her to delete Alex's numbers from her phone's contacts. She didn't wallow in Breakup Hell the way a moody Scorpio or Cancer would.

Cancer. That made me think of Sol. He didn't seem all that moody, but I didn't know him well. And that was the way it was going to stay.

The staff meeting was held in Stacy's office again. The foggy silver-gray skyline view of San Francisco filled the windows. Danielle, Stacy's tiny, intense assistant, brought in the coffee. Had I been promoted or demoted from caffeine duty? I didn't want to think about the answer to that question just then.

Bobby and Mary Elizabeth entered the room together. Bobby wore what appeared to be the same tired, wrinkled shorts he'd had on at the Terra High photo shoot. Mary Elizabeth was in what-looked like a hand-painted tee with gold streaks that matched her exquisite bob.

Most of the meeting was about money. How much the reception would cost. How much the models would cost. How much Alex Keen's wonderful food would cost. How much the celebrities posing with the high school girls would cost. Then we got around to what I had been waiting for. The photo shoot.

"So we have Zac, Jake, Ted, and maybe Rob, if he's in a good mood," Stacy said. "Who else?"

"Josh," Bobby called out. "Stace, he's still into Arianna. I know you can get him."

"Maybe. We'll see." She looked over at me. "You're our demographic, Logan. Who's your choice?"

"Cory." My voice broke. "Cory Scott, I mean."

"I love it." She screeched like a groupie at a concert. "Not even close to what I expected you to say, but Cory's perfect. He's so perfect."

"Forget that loser," Bobby shouted, in that braying, broad-chested way of his. "Cory is strictly B-list. Talented? Yes. Has-been? Also yes."

"Do you agree with that, Logan?" Stacy asked.

What did I know? "A lot of kids still listen to *Mellick*," I said. "And even though Arianna is the one who's really made it, Cory was the only one in the group who could write songs."

"But he's B-list, hon," Bobby said. "B-list all the way. What don't you get about that?"

Oh, great. Now I was in a battle with him. Too bad because I liked him, but I also liked Cory and knew this magazine shoot could be a great opportunity for him. "Actually," I said in my slowest, not-give-a-damn-est California speak, "you probably wouldn't understand. It's kind of a generational thing."

"Generational?" I'd pushed the Bull's buttons, all right, which meant only that he had buttons to push. "What the hell are you talking about? You think my age somehow scrambles my brain so I don't know a B-list freakin has-been when I see one?"

"Sorry." I glanced from him to Stacy, hoping for support. "I meant only that Cory Scott might have been finished—I mean, limited—professionally when Arianna left *Mellick*, but he still has a strong cult following."

"Not to mention, he's gorgeous," Mary Elizabeth put in. "And still so young. You and I always say that we can learn from these kids, Bobby, and this might be one of those times."

"Whatever." He gave me a not-so-friendly smile. "You made some good points, hon. And bottom line, we can argue right through lunch, but it all comes down to what our esteemed editor decides."

We all looked at Stacy. Her decision would determine Cory's future. For a moment, she didn't register any expression. Sitting at her desk in a short pink jacket that matched her lip gloss, she seemed to be thinking about how to respond.

"Well?" Bobby finally demanded.

"Well," she said, obviously parroting him. "I guess I have to agree with Logan. Cory is not B-list. He's the most talented of their old group, including Josh and Arianna."

"Meaning?" Bobby asked.

"Meaning, I think we should use Cory. I definitely think we should."

Something about the way she flushed when she said his name made my skin crawl. Then I realized what was going on. She wanted Cory to get this gig, and not because of me or what I wanted or cared about. No. She wanted him for herself.

NOTES TO SELF

Now that I think about it, I should have known better. Stacy set me up to lobby for Cory. Me, a nobody kid intern. Why? It's so simple that I should be slapped for not seeing it sooner—so that Stacy wouldn't have to do it herself. She has a thing for Cory. Let her have him. I never took his interest in me seriously anyway. I do want to keep Snider supporting my internship, though. When I asked—because I desperately needed to—about the judging process, Stacy told me that Graciela would review the photos from each school and select the girl she thought would best represent that school. It is all I need to please Snider and appease the few, I hope, weirdos who believe the garbage Kat, through her loyal servant, Dina, is spreading through the school.

18

ALWAYS EXPECT THE UNEXPECTED, AND KNOW THAT
SOME SIGNS HANDLE SURPRISE EVENTS BETTER THAN
OTHERS. ARIES BLAZES PAST ANY CHANGE OF PLANS.
TAURUS DOESN'T LIKE ANY SUDDEN ONES. GEMINI
HEADS FOR THE BACK BURNER AND PLAN B, C, AND
MAYBE EVEN D. CANCER RESISTS. LEO GETS BOSSY.
VIRGO WORRIES. LIBRA DELIBERATES. SCORPIO IGNORES.
SAGITTARIUS TALKS MORE. CAPRICORN WORKS MORE.
AQUARIUS THINKS MORE. PISCES WITHDRAWS MORE.

—Fearless Astrology

*I*t was true that I was thinking more, but it was all I could do just now. Finally, I had a chance to look at the ephemeris for the weekend of October 31. And, yes, I should have done it sooner. Arianna wasn't the only one who had a potential for disaster at that time. It appeared as though I had better be equally cautious. Not only was Fire sign Leo going to be squared, but Mars was going to be in Sagittarius, another Fire sign that would affect my Aries Rising. And maybe not in a good way.

As I sat there trying to digest the astrological warning glyphs early that morning, I received a text message from Cory.

Sorry. Have to take a date to the party. Still hope to see u there. CS.

Why was Cory—make that CS—apologizing to me? We had only planned to meet up there. And now, just after I had insisted that he should be in the magazine, he was telling me that he had to take someone to the party. The someone could be only one person. Stacy had found her King of Hearts, and I had helped seal the magazine deal. She had used me, and maybe he had too.

Mercury in Retro had taken its toll. Paige spilled Chai tea on her sketchbook. Chili had left her bag, books, and homework in journalism.

That morning Paige showed us the sketches of her Aphrodite costume. Even through the tea stains, the drawings were amazing. Looking at them, I could imagine that sleek, draped, and fitted gown with intricate braided cords and slits that revealed matching gladiator sandals. I tried to picture her in it and knew that it would be a Paige we had never seen before.

"It's beautiful," I said. "And you will be too."

"I just hope I can pull it off. It's the spirit and the soul of everything I want to show Graciela about my design abilities. I'm just wondering if I should ask someone else to wear it."

"You have to wear it," Chili said. "How else will Graciela know it's your design?"

"And there's no reason to get someone else involved." I ran my finger along one of the drawings. "You have the perfect shape for it, Paige."

"Make that lack of shape." But I could tell she was feeling more confident.

"A model's shape." Chili said. "Just suck in your cheeks, turn off your smile, and channel your inner bitch."

We were still talking about the dress when we got to school.

Dina waited for us in the parking lot. This time, Kat was with her. They wore matching white shirts and big own-the-world grins.

"Hi, Chili. Hi Paige. Hiiii…," Dina called out as if unable to turn off the one-word-fits-all-Terra High greeting machine.

"Dude," Chili interrupted, "what the hell is your problem? Or do you always hang out in parking lots? Never know who you might pick up there, do you?"

"You could teach us a lot about picking up guys, Chili." Aries Kat was in rare form. Pure Cardinal bitch. Her eyes had so much liner on them and so much mascara that it flaked in ugly chunks. I wondered how she could see around them.

"You'd better shut your mouth," I told her. "This isn't going to play out the way it did before. You aren't going to turn the school against me again."

"I don't even care about you right now, Logan."

"Good. Then get the hell out of our way," I said. "How pathetic, hanging out here waiting for us to show up."

"Pathetic is right." Chili gave her a look of pure disgust. "And before you go to class, you really ought to wash your face."

Paige and I exchanged looks. The bad Gemini twin had been unleashed.

Although clearly pissed, Kat continued to smile. I could only imagine how much she wanted to rub her finger under her eyes.

Instead she pointed her key at the monster of an SUV beside us. *Mega click.* Monster car was unlocked. Kat reached in.

"I have something of yours," she said and pulled out Chili's book bag.

"Where'd you steal that?" I asked.

"I didn't steal it." She grinned. "I found it in the journalism room. And, yeah, girls, I found more than I bargained for."

"Give it to me." Chili yanked it out of her hands.

"Oh, you can have it back now." Kat crossed her arms over her chest. "I've already taken everything I need. From your cell phone, I mean."

Chili's eyes grew wide, and she almost choked. "You slutty, little . . ."

"You should talk."

"What is it, Kat?" I demanded. "What are you trying to say?"

"Let your friend answer that one." Over her shoulder, Kat spelled out, "S-E-X."

"Chili?" I still couldn't figure out what was going on.

She seemed to melt. "You skank," she shouted to Kat. "You're the biggest bitch in school. You flash your ass and your tats all over town. You have no right to even attempt to . . ."

Kat smirked. "Tell me one time I ever sent my naked boobs to anyone."

"They weren't naked." Chili looked frantic now. "Big freaking deal."

"Sexting," she said. "Come on, Dina. We have a lot of work to do."

Paige and I turned to Chili. She blinked and tossed her hair. "It's not like I was naked or anything," she said, and burst into tears.

"How naked?" I whispered.

"I cropped the shot." She made a chopping movement across her front and then reached for the clump of tissues Paige handed her.

"Why didn't you tell us," Paige asked, in a pleading voice.

"Because I knew you'd tell me not to. I knew you'd tell me it was too dangerous." She wiped her eyes and turned her smeared face toward me. "Freaking Mercury in Retrograde. Oh, Logan, what am I going to do?"

NOTES TO SELF

I didn't have any easy answers for her, and neither did the stars. Kat and Dina played their game all day long. Soon everyone in school had a fine view of most of Chili's magnificent chest. The photo even showed up in Bodmer's class by way of Dina. Bodmer took her phone on the spot and sent both it and Dina to the Student Responsibility Center. At least that phone would stay there until one of Dina's parents picked it up.

Tonight, Chili tried to explain it to Paige and me that Alex was the only guy for her. Since he was older and more sophisticated, she wanted him to have something special. He had asked for a really personal commitment and had even sent some photos of himself to her. Thankfully, she had deleted them before Kat got hold of her phone.

So now we have a couple of problems. The first is Chili's attractive upper and very bare chest being shared around school. The second is will this little social error keep her from being able to attend the magazine launch party? I don't know. All I know is that Mercury is in Retrograde and communication and technical errors are going to be common. In a way, Chili's situation is both. And Mercury is Gemini's ruling planet. It's going to be double trouble for her this time.

CRUSHES: HOW TO INTRIGUE A SCORPIO
By Logan McRae

That Scorpio guy is probably one of the most passionate ones you will ever meet. Passionate about what he wears to school. Passionate about what he eats for lunch. Passionate about whom he dates, and, most of all, passionate about his past. He may not be happy about his role and responsibilities in his family, but he'll be passionate about them as well.

To get him looking at you, don't ask many questions. Unlike the chatty Air signs, he'll hold back at first, and only tell you when he's ready. Or maybe never.

Here are three ways to intrigue him:

*• **Demonstrate trust.** That Scorpion isn't going to come one step closer unless you show that you're someone safe. Translated, someone who can keep his secrets. Refuse to discuss any school gossip that involves a friend. Make, "That's a confidence I can't break," your new favorite mantra. Don't spill personal info, and that Scorpio will soon be looking your way.*

• **Share intensity.** *When the weather cooperates, tell him how much you enjoy a rainstorm. Suggest that the two of you watch it together. Scorpio doesn't mind if you make the first move.*

• **Stay separate and independent.** *Make it clear that, as much as you are into him, you have your own life and your own interests. Scorpio doesn't want to be joined at the hip from day one.*

What to say when he asks you out: *"Let's go someplace quiet where we can just talk."*

19

PISCES IS THE LAST SIGN OF THE ZODIAC, AND SOMETIMES CAN TAKE UP THE REAR IN LIFE, AS WELL. A FISH MAY BE WILLING TO STAY IN AN UNREWARDING RELATIONSHIP, BUSINESS OR PERSONAL, JUST BECAUSE IT IS EASIER THAN TAKING A STAND. LIKE WATER RELATIONS CANCER AND SCORPIO, PISCES CAN ELEVATE SELF-SACRIFICE TO AN ART FORM. SOMETIMES, PISCES, YOU NEED TO TAKE A DEEP BREATH AND PUT YOURSELF FIRST.

—*Fearless Astrology*

*I*t could have been worse. Even though Chili got dragged across the River Styx into Dr. West's office, and even though her mom got called, she was still going to be able to attend the launch party. Her rescuer happened to be Bodmer, who said to all who would listen, what an outstanding and serious student Chili was.

Once class was out, we were all going to sleep over at Chili's house, and then head for San Fran early the next morning. They had volunteered to do extra credit work so that they could take the day off.

"Ready?" I asked, as we walked to the parking lot that afternoon.

"I don't know." Chili ran her fingers through her hair. "How can I face Alex after what happened?"

"Alex has no idea what or even if anything happened," I said. "Why tell him?"

"Because . . . because. Oh, I don't know. I just like to tell the truth."

"Gemini flaw." I put up my hand. "He doesn't need to know, okay?"

"Logan knows what she's talking about." We both stopped to stare at Paige. It wasn't so much the way she looked that had changed, although it had. Right now, it was about her voice. She no longer seemed to speak in her usual shy, stumbling, start-stop way.

"Right in what way?" Chili asked.

"In that he doesn't need to know. He being Alex."

"Listen to us for once," I said. "Why let him start

wondering if you could be trouble?"

"You girls are so smart." She stopped and hugged us both. "I just don't know how to handle myself with an older guy. I am just so into him."

"That's for sure," Paige said.

"I never would have done what I did otherwise. I never have before. It's like something Kat would do. I feel like such an idiot."

For a brief moment, I wondered if I would have had a happier ending to my true love story if I had sent Jeremy a sexy photo or two. "It's all right, Chili," I said. "At least you get to attend the party."

"They couldn't keep me away."

"This is our moment." Paige put her arms around both of us. "We'll get past the sexting thing, and tomorrow, girls, we are going to own that party."

"Yeah we are. We have the best costumes on the . . ." Chili stopped. "My window," she cried out. "What the hell happened to my window?"

Then I saw it. The passenger side window of her car was smashed. We all ran toward it.

"Who would do this?" Chili demanded. "I've got to call my dad."

Then I looked into the backseat. At the shreds of her costume, her broken mask.

"Let's go report this," I said. But it was too late. Chili had also seen the mess. And she was sobbing.

"It has to be Kat, that jealous little bitch. Or Dina. Or both of them."

"Let's go to the vice principal, Chili, right now."

"What good will that do? My costume is in shreds. Where am I going to find something else to wear?"

"She's right, Logan." Paige also seemed to be near tears. "We can report what happened when we get back. Right now, we have to figure out a costume for Chili. And we have to do it before we leave tomorrow morning."

"Is there any way you can fix it?" I looked at the ripped-up fabric, the shattered mask, and knew the answer.

Paige shook her head slowly, and her blue eyes shimmered with tears. "All of that work," she said. "All of that time."

"Could you do something edgy? Maybe pretend it's supposed to be ripped and wear it over tights."

"Logan, it's Catwoman. Her vibe isn't goth. It's straight-on sex appeal."

"We'll figure out something," I said. "Come on, you guys. Let's go shopping and make a new Catwoman for Chili."

"It's my fault." Paige hadn't moved. "I never should have brought it to school. I should have known better than to leave in the car."

"It's not your fault." Chili squeezed her arm. "Come on, Paige. Logan's plan might not be perfect, but it's the only plan we have. We're going to have to put together a new costume with whatever we can find."

She straightened and crossed her arms in front of her chest. "It won't work. You're going to have to wear my costume."

"Aphrodite?" Chili asked. "I can't do that."

"You have the body for it. I can make the alterations

tonight. It's my fault this happened in the first place."

"But what about you? If I'm Aphrodite, who are you going to be?"

"I'll figure it out while I'm doing the alterations on the costume." Paige reached for the car door as if to say that had settled it.

I couldn't let her continue to be a Pisces doormat.

"Wait a minute," I said. "You've done this since we were in elementary school."

"Done what?"

"Our homework, for starters. You've always taken a backseat to us, literally." I tapped the door of the car. "Pisces can be loyal and creative. They can also be willing to take up the rear, and sometimes they even wear self-sacrifice like a freaking badge. You can't do it this time, Paige. Graciela Perez can change your life. You have got to wear that costume."

"But what about Chili?"

"I'll be fine." The Gemini had bounced back again. She flashed me a look that said she was in agreement. Then she climbed inside the car. "Come on, girls. We've got some shopping to do."

NOTES TO SELF

This has been one of the craziest nights of my life. We hit the local craft store and grabbed anything that had the remotest Catwoman vibe. No more tears. We were out of victim mode and on a mission now.

Paige still had leftover fabric from the original costume, including a long, narrow piece of black satin she had draped around Calypso, her wrought-iron mannequin that had seen us through some pretty scary times in the past. Finally, Chili stood before us as what Paige called a "minimalist Catwoman," from satin ears and metallic tail to long black nails and huge false eyelashes. We are going to have to do the rest with makeup and Chili's Gemini attitude. In six hours, we have to leave for San Francisco.

As I said, it's been one of the craziest nights. And tomorrow is going to be even crazier.

CRUSHES: HOW TO TAME A SADGE
By Logan McRae

Almost everyone loves Sagittarius. He's frequently laughing and almost always has a smile on his face. No wonder so many girls are attracted to him. This sign is what's known as expansive in astro speak. All that means is that he's full of ideas, dreams, and optimism. Maybe even a little full of himself, but not in a bad way.

As you may have noticed, he's not attracted to anyone who tries to kill his dreams, criticize his game plan, or whine about their own problems. Although you probably won't be the first girl he's ever dated, there are ways to make yourself stand out to this Fire sign.

Here are three:

• **Be positive.** *The Archer loves someone to cheer him on. Tell him that you have goals and dreams of your own. Make it clear that you respect and are excited about his goals. He'll feel the same way about yours.*

• **Forget the past.** *He may have dated every girl in every school and neighboring community within fifty miles of where you live. That doesn't mean that you won't matter. You just won't matter at first.*

• **Refuse to fall.** *Because you won't matter right away, you can't cave in, let alone hook up, the first time he gives you that forever look. Make it fun. Make it friendship, with a possible promise of more. If you fall fast, you're almost sure to lose this guy. Too many girls have already fallen fast for him.*

What to say when he asks you out: *"This is going to be such fun."*

20

WHEN YOU FIND YOURSELF IN UNFAMILIAR TERRI-
TORY, DRAW UPON THE STRENGTH OF YOUR SUN SIGN.
IF YOU ARE FIRE (ARIES, LEO, SAGITTARIUS), BE FEAR-
LESS. IF YOU ARE EARTH (TAURUS, VIRGO, CAPRI-
CORN), BE STEADY AND STRONG. IF YOU ARE AIR
(GEMINI, LIBRA, AQUARIUS), ASK QUESTIONS, COM-
MUNICATE. IF YOU ARE WATER (CANCER, SCORPIO,
PISCES), RELY ON YOUR INTUITION.

—Fearless Astrology

Ask questions. I needed to remember that today. It was
still dark when we arrived in the city. Chili's dad had
given us a loaner to drive. And to Andy Chiliderian, a
BMW was just that. He was furious about the damage to

Chili's Spyder and maybe even more so about what had happened to her costume. Andy adored his only daughter, and I knew whoever broke into the car would be in big trouble.

"It had to be Kat and Dina," Chili said. "No one else hates us like that."

"You never know," I told her. "Since I found that astrology book last spring, I've learned a lot about being hated."

"Make that being envied," Chili said, and glanced in the rearview mirror. "Paigie, I am so glad you are going to be wearing the Aphrodite costume."

Like most Geminis, she was a nickname person. But she hadn't called Paige that since middle school.

"You're okay with your own costume, aren't you?" I asked her.

"Thanks to you two, I can pull it off. Who knows? Maybe Alex is into minimalist."

Alex is into you. That's what she wanted me to say and what I wished I could say, but I couldn't. He was a wandering too-old Sadge, and I had witnessed his wandering in a certain hotel not so long ago.

Silence filled the car louder than music, even Arianna Woods's music, which is what happened to be playing. So Paige must feel the same way I did about Alex. The only difference was that I had a reason neither of them knew about.

"I really care about him," Chili said.

"I know," I said. "Sometimes really caring can suck."

"It doesn't suck for me." She continued looking straight ahead. "Have you ever considered that the reason you distrust Alex so much is because of Jeremy's disappearing act?"

"Chili," Paige said. "Please, let's not go there."

"Chili is right." Just like that, I knew I had been avoiding what had been clear to everyone else. "Jeremy has dumped me, and I just can't accept it. Once I finally called, all I got was his answering machine, with a girl's voice on it."

"He found someone in Ireland?"

"She didn't sound Irish. But she was on his phone."

"Call him again," Chili said.

"You need to find out." Paige squeezed my shoulder from the backseat. "It could have been his sister."

"He doesn't have a sister," I said.

"Well then, maybe you should call him."

I knew Paige was right. Knew Chili was right. But I was still as much in love with Jeremy as I had been in Monterey. My friends were basically telling me to choose between my fantasy of love and reality. I couldn't keep pretending.

"Okay, here goes." I took out my phone and pressed the keypad.

The phone's ringing sounded like chimes. Once. Twice. Then, "Hi. This is Tori."

It was the same voice I had heard before, and it made me feel sick, cold, and clammy all over.

"Could I speak to Jeremy?"

"Who's calling?"

"Um, may I just speak to Jeremy."

"I asked you who's calling. I'm his girlfriend. Who are you?"

"Logan," I said. "His other girlfriend."

For a moment, I felt the world freeze between us.

"Logan?" She paused. "He was supposed to tell you." Her voice was soft now, almost a whisper, but I could still hear the pity in it. "Didn't he tell you that we're together now? I'm so sorry. I . . ."

My phone went dead.

So did I.

"Is it bad?" Chili finally asked.

"Bad," I said. But I didn't cry. "Let's talk about it later, okay? We have enough to deal with right now."

"Logan, you have to tell us."

"I can't," I said, cold all over now, frozen to the bone. "Let's just say that the mystery is solved, and I no longer have a boyfriend."

So now I knew for sure what I had suspected all along. Jeremy had found someone else and hadn't cared enough to let me know. I couldn't deal with it yet, though. Chili dropped me off at the hotel. From there, they would go to the Chiliderians' place in the Embarcadero. I wouldn't see them again until they walked in, fully costumed, tonight. And in Chili's case, minimally costumed. But Paige could perform miracles, and Chili could pull off just about anything.

"I know you'll both look hot," I said. "You already do."

"So do you." Paige hugged me. "Don't feel bad. You've got a killer costume and friends who love you."

"I really do like my Sherlock," I told her.

"You work that Sherlock. It rocks." She gave me a conspiring Pisces grin. "And you were right about what you said.

You know, how I always take up the rear. I'm warning you right now that if Graciela likes my costume, I'm riding home in the front seat on Sunday."

"You're going to ride up there anyway," I said, "regardless of what happens."

My friends. I watched them pull away into that fine, chaotic energy of San Francisco. I could get through this breakup with Jeremy. Somehow, I would do it. And tonight, I'd work my Sherlock, and no one, not even my best friends, would know what was going on inside me.

"Hey, Logan."

I turned to see a girl in jeans, an oversized *Mellick* tee and a baseball cap. No makeup, but I had no problem recognizing Arianna.

"Hey." I said. "You look like everyone else."

"That's the point." She rushed up to me. "I just got here."

"Me too." She looked sober. That was a good thing.

"Aren't you with someone?" I asked. Where were her people? I was certain they would have her on a short leash today.

"Dude. I'm with the only person I need to be with." She smiled with such hope that I felt like hugging her.

"Josh?" I remembered how it felt to believe the way she must be right now. How had I ever gotten more cynical than Arianna Woods?

"He's the one. You were right about Gemini and Capricorn. We're working it out."

"You can handle the Earth sign of Capricorn," I said, "Especially with that Aries Moon of yours. He can calm you down."

"Aries Moon?" she asked. "Where'd you come up with that?"

"Your astrology chart," I said. "You have an Aries Moon, don't you?"

She shook her head. "Based on that astro stuff you told me to check out, my Moon is in Leo. Which explains why I like performing so much, right? And makes Josh and me an even better match."

For a moment, I couldn't figure out how to reply to her. Then I asked, "How do you know that your Moon is in Leo, Arianna?"

"Dude, because it just is. Want to see my chart?"

"No," I said. "I believe you."

"Well, I owe you. Until that day we talked, I knew my Sun sign, but that was about it. Now . . ." That blissed-out expression again.

"My offer is still good," I told her. "If you want me to do a compatibility chart for you and Josh, I mean."

"I'll let you know if we need one." She gave me that in-love look again. "We'd better get up there. The service elevator is busted again, but the regular one is okay. No one's going to recognize me."

"You use the service elevator?" I asked, remembering Alex Keen, and that night in the hotel that I had watched him go into her room.

"Oh, yeah." She pulled the cap down over her eyes and shoved some strands up into it. "Dude, I'll be okay. Just stay close to me. Josh promised to meet me upstairs. I understand what you were trying to tell me about him. He's an

Earth sign, and I love his stability. He makes me feel safe."

"Good." That was about all I could say to her Air sign barrage of words.

The elevator dinged. No one seemed to be paying any attention to us, so, the moment the doors opened, we stepped inside.

"Look." She turned and pulled down her jeans. There, on the tanned rise of her butt, was a tattoo, a V-shape, but the right side swirled into a kind of spiral. Of course. It was a glyph of the Capricorn goat.

"Cool," I said.

"I have Gemini on the other side. Check it out."

"Later," I said. "The door's going to open any second. Are those new?"

Good for me. I'd lost the boy I loved but had another astro convert. Make that Gemini astro convert. The problem was, that was all I had. I had been tricked into thinking Arianna was the one in danger. Now, all I could think about, as I pretended to admire her tattooed testimonial to Josh, was that I had been worried about the wrong Gemini.

The wrong Gemini. That was it. Arianna wasn't the double Gem with the Aries Moon. Actually, her Moon was in Leo.

So who was the in-trouble Gem with the Aries Moon? I had a pretty good idea. And I really should have figured it out sooner than this.

CRUSHES: HOW TO ENTICE A CAPRICORN

By Logan McRae

Cool and sometimes standoffish, that Capricorn Mountain Goat has a dry wit and a strong need to succeed. Wouldn't it be fun if you could distract him from his tedious Earth sign duties of studying and responsibilities and make him go a little crazy about you for a change? You can.

Even when he's wearing his oldest pair of jeans or up to his elbows in grease, this guy is elegance personified. There's just something about him that makes you want to stand straighter and dress your best. That's a good way to start.

Entice that creature. True, he's sometimes a status seeker, but once you get to know him, you'll realize he's only into that plan of being a doctor or politician or chemist or TV news anchor because he was denied something as a child. Money. Love. Mommy. It doesn't matter. He has a direction now, a clear path paved with hard work, and no one will stand in his way.

That doesn't rule you out, though. Here are three ways to make him forget about work and focus on you (at least for the short term):

• **Care.** *This sign has committed to major goals and needs major feedback. Recognize even the smallest accomplishments. "How'd you ever get that grade in her class?" "You studied how many hours last night?" "And with a part-time job, you did, what?"*

• **Share.** *He has a goal. You have a goal. Perhaps yours is in a sport or drama or student government. Share your ambition. Demonstrate that you are also someone, who like him, wants more out of life, and someone who is willing to work for it.*

• **Don't despair.** *A sure way to appeal to this sign is when things go wrong for him. Move in close when that happens. Take charge, if you must. Don't entertain a negative thought, and don't let him entertain one. Remind him, in a subtle way, that he is not alone.*

What to say when he asks you out: *"What about Friday? It's my only night off this week."*

21

YOUR SUN SIGN IS WHAT YOU ARE, AND YOUR ASCEN-
DANT (RISING) SIGN IS WHAT PEOPLE SEE. THE MOON
COLORS AND INFLUENCES THE TRAITS. BE CAREFUL
WHEN GUESSING SIGNS. IT IS EASY TO SEE THE MOON'S
INFLUENCE AND BELIEVE IT IS THE SUN SIGN. DON'T
MAKE THIS MISTAKE.

—*Fearless Astrology*

hat's what I had done. I had guessed a Sun sign based on
observed behavior. And I had done it more than once.
Stacy, not Arianna, was the Gemini with the Aries
Moon. I had ignored the obvious communication skills and
focused on her need for success. She wasn't a spotlight-grab-
bing Leo. She was a Fire-influenced Gemini eager to take on
any task she was handed. And her need for success was really

a desire to be admired and to have the world revolve around her. Some astrologer I was. I had picked up on her Aries Moon and completely missed her Gemini Sun.

I found her in the kitchen. She had pulled her dark hair back and tied it with a multicolored scarf. At first she didn't notice me, too busy walking through the place with Bobby, the art director, who had finally changed into some khakis and a pale green shirt. He carried a plastic Jack in the Box head, which I feared he actually planned to wear. But maybe not. Maybe it was just his idea of California atmosphere.

Already the musicians' stage had been set up, already the stations for appetizers and alcohol. Soon the costumed guests would begin arriving. I followed Bobby and Stacy into the large banquet room overlooking the city.

"Hi, Stacy," I said. "Have a minute?"

"Sorry, but there's just too much to do right now. Let's chat soon."

"I don't want to chat," I told her.

"What then?"

"I'd like to talk." I said it with such force that I actually got her attention.

"I have five minutes, no more." She glanced back at Bobby, and I realized how wound up she was. "Let's go outside."

The foggy air on the balcony was cool and sharp, the skyline smoky.

"What do you want?" she asked.

"Why did you lie to me about Arianna's sign?"

She grabbed the rail and glared at me. "I never said it was hers."

"And more important, you never said it was your sign. But it is yours, isn't it?"

"You're way out of line here, Logan. As much as I respect Henry, you're a little too weird with this astro stuff, and I'm not telling you anything else."

"You don't have to," I said. "I know you're the double Gemini with the Aries Moon."

"What are you talking about?"

"Gemini Sun, Gemini Rising. Aries Moon. That's the chart you gave me to figure out. You need to listen to me, and you also need to figure out a way to stop this party. If you don't, something terrible is going to happen."

"That's ridiculous," Stacy said. "The party is on, and no one can stop it. I've had enough of this." She turned away from the rail, her expression icy. "Now, I need to go change into my costume. I owe your shy little friend for that one. Remind me to thank her."

NOTES TO SELF

Although Stacy refused to cancel the party, she did give me what I wanted. Except now that she's confirmed that she's the Gemini who's going to be in trouble, I'm more worried than ever. Because I think Stacy is right. I think it is probably too late to cancel anything, including what is in the stars.

CRUSHES: HOW TO ATTRACT AN AQUARIUS

By Logan McRae

The Aquarius cutie is one of the most fascinating creatures in the zodiac. He has strong opinions and ideas about the way the world does and should work. Even though he is an Air sign, he is Fixed Air. This guy doesn't gush. He ponders before offering his input. He may be so lost in his own world that he hasn't even noticed that you exist. Time to change that.

You can spot him in a classroom. He's the guy with the twinkly eyes and the weird hair, who after everyone else has talked a subject to death, raises his hand and quietly makes the most brilliant point of all.

He has no interest in girls who go with the flow. If you stand out from the crowd, you'll have the best chance of attracting him. That means in dress and attitude, and most of all, in the causes you care about. Cute but brainless chicks hold no appeal for him. Nor do those who try to hit on him in the usual ways.

Here are three ways to get his head out of the clouds and his mind focused on you:

• **Have a social conscience.** *This isn't something you can fake. You really do have to care. If your only outside interest is getting your nails done, move on down the zodiac and find yourself a nice Aries or Leo. Do you volunteer in the kitchen of the local homeless shelter? Do you help register voters? If you are involved not just in yourself, but in the world around you, Aquarius will notice.*

• **Listen.** *This sign loves to talk about his causes. If he feels that you are with him, he may go on and on. That brilliant Aquarius mind just doesn't stop. Don't interrupt him to demonstrate how brilliant you are. He isn't doing this to impress you, and he doesn't want you to try to impress him. He's sharing what's in his head.*

• **Give him space.** *If you don't give it to him, he'll take it anyway. He may be late to pick you up because something important sidetracked him. This doesn't mean he's not into you. He's not a flirt or a two-timer. He may forget to call—or once he does—come across as hesitant or shy on the phone. Ask questions, but don't push. He knows what he wants.*

What to say when he asks you out: *"There's an Earth Day planning meeting going on that night. Want to come along?"*

22

YOUR ASTROLOGICAL CHART IS A MAP THAT WAS BORN THE MOMENT YOU WERE. IT IS A GUIDE TO YOUR STRENGTHS AND CHALLENGES, AND ON OCCASION, THE TIMES OF YOUR GREATEST DURESS. TRAGEDY BEFALLS US ALL. SOONER OR LATER, WE ALL MUST DEAL WITH ENEMIES, SOME MORE THREATENING THAN OTHERS. CHOOSE YOUR ENEMIES CAREFULLY. WHEN YOU KNOW THEIR ASTROLOGICAL CHARTS AS WELL AS YOU KNOW YOUR OWN, YOU WILL PREVAIL.

—Fearless Astrology

The Gemini night had finally arrived. Dusk had settled over the city, transforming it to a living lithograph of gray, black, and white. I tried to forget the sound of

Jeremy's girlfriend's voice on the phone. He was a supposed-to-be-true Taurus. How had I lost him so soon? Francis, the angry chef, had told me that I could change in the staff restroom. That made me like him better. Besides, I could see that he loved his kitchen. It couldn't be fun to have Alex taking it over and treating him like an assistant.

Once I had finished putting on my Sherlock, I looked into the mirror and had to admire myself in the short skirt and cool hat. The pockets were deep, so it was easy to stash my pipe, cell phone, and notebook.

The door swung open. Two women in black dresses and sequined face masks flew in like crows.

"Sherlock," one of them said. "You go."

At least she had recognized who I was supposed to be. I couldn't help wondering why they were in the staff restroom, but I couldn't obsess about that right now. It was time to join the party.

With the wide windows reflecting the lights of the city, it seemed as if the night had come inside. I stepped out of the elevator and tried to pretend that I wasn't buzzing with anxiety, fear, and a major broken heart.

The rooftop hotel ballroom was filled with everyone from Tarzan, Cleopatra, Marie Antoinette, Shrek, Princess Leia, Spider-Man, and Wonder Woman. Sweeney Todd and Mrs. Lovett mingled with Napoleon and Josephine. Flavor Flav, with a clock around his neck, flashed his grill and adjusted his Viking horns as he checked out Stacy in her Queen of Hearts gown.

Behind her was the tall, muscular King of Hearts, long dark hair pulled back behind a red-and-gold hat trimmed in fake ermine. Paige hadn't had time to help Cory with the design of his costume, and it showed. The same fake ermine trimmed the sides and bottom of his matching red coat. A mask covered most of his face, but I knew that the eyes would be blue trimmed with thick, dark lashes.

When he saw me, he turned away, and I wondered if he was embarrassed for me to see him dressed up in a matchy-matchy version of Stacy's costume. He'd done this, I knew, so that he could be in the magazine to resurrect his career.

A string quartet played at a low volume at one end of the suite, but the laughter and conversations among the guests drowned out the music. No wonder the magazine had rented and closed off the block of rooms below us. No one down there would be able to sleep tonight.

Just then, Henry Jaffa walked in. One look, and I knew he was supposed to be Edgar Allan Poe, complete with the black velvet raven perched upon the shoulder of his topcoat. He caught my eye and grinned. Finally, I had a friend here. I ran up to him.

"That's an original costume," he said, "and appropriate. How's it going?"

"I'm worried," I said. "Something bad is going to happen tonight."

"Are you speaking from an astrological perspective?" he asked.

I nodded. "More than that, though. I tried to talk to Stacy

about it."

"She mentioned that there had been some . . ." I could see him try to search for an appropriate term. ". . . some tension between you two. I was sorry to hear that. She's been very successful at a very young age and could be an excellent role model for you."

"She's been dishonest with me from the start," I said. "Remember when she gave me the astrological chart to figure out? She said it was the chart of a celebrity who would be attending the party. Only it was her chart, and there's what we call a square, a potential for disaster for her tonight. She won't listen to me."

"What sort of disaster?" I could see that I had his attention now.

"I don't know. The stars aren't that exact."

"Then there's not much we can do," he said. "And what if you're wrong? You know that you'll lose Stacy's respect and the magazine astrology column right along with it."

"I know that, but I don't think I'm wrong."

At that moment, Josh Mellick stepped into the room. He was dressed as both Dr. Jekyll and Mr. Hyde, and his costume was half lab coat, half tuxedo tails, half professor mask, half ghoul. Gemini Arianna must have picked it out. He was even better looking than his photos. His teeth were so white I knew he must be seriously into bleach strips, and I could see the famous spiked hair over the top of his mask.

Arianna walked in behind him, no more baseball cap and jeans. In her '90s Madonna costume, complete with cone bra, she looked like the star she was. Capricorn Josh could be a good sign for her. I hoped, for her sake, that it worked out. Like most Gemini Sun signs, she had two sides, and I still didn't know what she'd been doing with Alex that night.

The elevator opened. Catwoman slinked in alone. She was cute yet edgy with the super lashes and long, black whiskers painted on her face. Then came Aphrodite. I barely recognized Paige. Without her glasses and her pale hair pulled straight back and topped by a wreath of burnished leaves, she was beyond beautiful. Now I realized how smart she had been to forego wearing a mask. That face was all she needed.

How much of beauty was attitude? I wondered. Although she had the same features as regular old Paige, she didn't look anything like that girl.

I started toward them, one so sexy and the other so stunning. Then I glanced over at the top of the stairs beside the elevator. There stood a slender, golden-skinned woman in an aluminum miniskirt and a mass of hair the same color. She inhaled slowly, as if breathing in the room. Once she spotted Paige, she paused, then boldly approached her.

"Your costume," she said. "Who designed it?"

"I did, Graciela."

Graciela. The Platinum Dragon. She was here, and she was actually speaking to Paige.

"You designed it? Then, you are very talented, my friend. You have, perhaps, a mentor, someone older, who maybe guided you?"

"Paige is a design major," I said. "Isn't she, Chili?"

"She loves your beachwear." Chili flashed her a killer

smile, and the whiskers Paige had drawn onto her face broke into dimples.

"I have followed your work since I was a kid," Paige said, speaking over our words. "I love the way that all of your fabrics are cut on the bias. And those iridescent tones." She spoke with a confidence I had never seen in her before.

"We must talk," Graciela said. "But first tell me, please. Where is Arianna? I designed her Madonna costume, you know."

"She's right there." I turned to point her out, but Madonna was nowhere to be found. It was as if she had melted into the crowd.

NOTES TO SELF

Madonna has disappeared. I seem to be the only one who cares. Paige and Graciela are speaking the mysterious language of fashion design. Chili has moved, as if hypnotized, to Alex Keen, her Batman of the blond curls. But Madonna—Arianna is gone. And now that I think about it, so is Josh in his Jekyll and Hyde. Something's wrong. I know it is. But I have no idea what to do.

23

WHEN YOU ARE UNCERTAIN WHICH ACTION TO TAKE,
YOU MUST REMEMBER WHO YOU ARE. WHAT IS YOUR
STRENGTH? FIRE IS AGGRESSIVE. EARTH IS STABLE. AIR
IS ANALYTICAL. WATER IS EMOTIONAL. BUT ALL SIGNS
HAVE THAT INNATE GIFT OF FLYING, MOVING, THINK-
ING, OR FEELING THEIR WAY INTO ACTION IN TIMES OF
CRISES. YOU CAN DO THAT, WHATEVER YOUR SIGN.

—Fearless Astrology

had read that earlier today when I was hoping for any
message that would make sense to me. Remembering it
just then, I knew that my strength was all in this pondering
head of mine. And this pondering head insisted that I needed
to find Madonna. Needed to find Arianna. Even though Stacy
was the Gemini who was supposed to be in danger, something

was going on with Arianna, and I was worried about her.

I would start my search in that tiny area off the party room. It was reserved for the catering people, and although Alex Keen's staff dashed in and out of it, no one stayed for long. The tiny room smelled of garlic, cilantro, and something piercingly sweet. Ginger, maybe. Cinnamon. But no one was there. Then I saw it. A large square door in the wall. Another entrance to the service elevator.

"Oh no." I said it before I realized that I was talking to myself.

"Get me out of here." It was a low-pitched moan, and it was coming from the louvered doors of the pantry to my left. I opened it and found Josh, partially in and partially out of his Jekyll and Hyde costume, the mask around his neck.

"What's going on?" I asked him. "Who did this to you?"

"I don't know. I didn't see the guy." He rubbed his spiky hair, and I caught sight of the dried blood there.

"Where is Arianna?" I asked.

"I don't know. Someone just hit me from behind."

"But why?" The Capricorn knew more than he was telling me. "Why would anyone want to hit you?"

"Because of Arianna," he said. "Because of what she had planned."

"Tell me. The only way we can help her is if I know what's going on."

"I guess it doesn't matter now. Might as well tell you." He sighed. "She was going to fake her own kidnapping tonight."

"What are you talking about? Why would she do that?"

"To revive her career, of course. She told me at the last

minute. That was her plan."

My mind buzzed. "And you let her go through with it?"

"I didn't know it until just a few minutes ago. As soon as she told me, I said she had to stop it. We got into an argument, and that's when whoever it was hit me from behind. Someone really has taken her."

"We've got to find her," I said.

He rubbed his head again and winced. "Where do you think she is?"

"I'm starting with the ballroom," I told him. "If she isn't there, maybe I can find someone who saw her."

"I'll go with you." He stopped. "I owe you. I don't know what you did with that astro stuff, but you're the one who made her realize that she still loves me."

"She always has," I said. "I hope you two work it out."

I rushed into the ballroom. Not far from me, Madonna/Arianna stood by one of the champagne bars. When she saw me, she started to leave the room, but I followed her all the way to the exit.

"Leave me alone," she said. "Get out of here." It wasn't Arianna's voice.

I reached out and ripped off her mask. It wasn't Arianna who looked back at me, either. It was Stacy, pale skin tinged pink.

"What's going on?" I demanded.

"Nothing," she said. "Arianna and I switched costumes for fun. That's all."

I was starting to realize that nothing these two did was for fun.

"You switched so that people would think she's still at the party, didn't you? Where is she really?"

"How would I know?" Her cheeks were scarlet now. "I can't find her anywhere, and I just hope nothing happened to her."

"Something did happen to her," I said. "Someone knocked Josh out and took her."

"Are you sure? Why?"

"Yes, I'm sure, but I don't know," I said. "Josh told me she was trying to fake a kidnapping."

"That's ridiculous. Why would she do that?"

"For publicity? Public sympathy? Maybe to get back some of the respect she's lost. We need to call the police," I said. "Where's Henry Jaffa?"

I spotted him, the velvet raven still on his shoulder, in a conversation with a chubby Sweeney Todd in his top hat, long coat, and red cummerbund. Mrs. Lovett stood between them. She wore a black-and-white dress. Her silver-blond wig was a cascade of curls. Then I realized it was Bobby and Mary Elizabeth, the magazine's art and fashion directors. I didn't want to run up to them like a hysterical kid, but that was the way I felt right now. Jaffa would know what to do. I crossed the room and headed toward him.

"Could I speak with you for a moment?" I asked him.

He took one look at me and said, "What's wrong?"

"Arianna's been kidnapped," I whispered.

"Kidnapped? How? Tell me what happened."

"I will," I said, "but first we need to call the police, and we need to search the building."

As frightened as I was, I knew that I had been right all along about what I had predicted. I had also been right about the signs who were in the greatest danger—Gemini Stacy and Aquarius me.

Jaffa went to call the police, and the party continued, the costumed guests unaware of what was taking place. Stacy stood frozen clutching a glass of red wine. She had removed her Madonna mask, and her lips were a thin, tight line.

I approached her, and she turned away toward the windows and the reflected lights of the city.

"You and Arianna planned this together," I said. "Didn't you?"

"That's ridiculous, and so are you."

"Come on, Stacy. She wouldn't do this alone, and not just because she's a Gemini. She needed your help. Now the police are coming. You'd better turn this around, if you can."

"There's nothing to turn around." Her lip trembled. "You can't prove that I had anything to do with it."

"Josh can," I lied. "And he will. Arianna told him what you were planning."

"She wouldn't do that. No one's going to believe him."

She struggled to maintain her composure, but I saw the fear in her eyes. Aries Moon. That need to be in charge, to do it her way, whatever the consequences. It was what I had first noticed about her. But I had mistakenly thought her Moon was in Leo.

"Why'd you do it?" I asked. "Was it all about publicity you hoped to get for the magazine?"

"You have no idea of the pressure on me," she said. "*CRUSH* had to be a success from the start, and it will be now. You and Josh can say whatever you want. I'll just deny it."

"Who else knows what you were planning?"

"No one."

Such a Gemini. And such a rotten liar.

"Tell me the truth. Arianna shared it with Josh. What about you? Who'd you tell?"

Her face was stark white, her blush like pink blotches on her cheeks. "He wouldn't."

Cory. I knew she had told him. The guilt was all over her. I realized I was still holding the stupid Sherlock magnifying glass and shoved it back into my pocket.

"When was the last time you saw him?" I asked her.

"I'm not sure. I think he was going into the catering room. How could he have gotten her out of the building?"

"I intend to find out."

I hurried toward the catering room, with Stacy following right behind me. The service elevator was stopped at the floor below us, the floor that had been closed off tonight.

"I don't think he took her out of the building," I said.

"He wouldn't be crazy enough to stay here."

"On a closed-off floor? I'm not so sure. I'm going down there. Tell Henry Jaffa where I am."

"Don't go. It's too dangerous."

My days of taking orders from Stacy were over. I headed for the stairs, head spinning.

What if I was right? What if Cory had actually kidnapped Arianna? His interest in Stacy must have been as much of a sham as his interest in me. The only difference was that Stacy had been clueless enough to believe him, confide in him, and probably to fall for him.

It would be too risky for him to leave the building with Arianna. And the service elevator was stopped at the eleventh floor. He had to be hiding out on the floor beneath the noisy activities of the party. That's probably why Chili and I had gotten stuck in the service elevator that Friday with Alex Keen. Cory must have shut it down while he was setting up what he planned to do. What would happen to Arianna? I had to find her before any more time escaped.

I ran down the stairs to the next floor. When I got there, I looked both ways down the coral carpet. Nothing. The floor was like a tomb. I wanted to run back the way I had come, but I knew Arianna had to be here. Held by a Scorpio who must not have been able to get over her or the way she had deserted him and their group.

"Arianna," I shouted. "Where are you?"

Nothing.

"Arianna, I know you're here. Cory, you'd better let her go. Jaffa's already called the police."

"Help." No mistaking Arianna's voice.

I followed the hall to my right, and then I saw an open door. Arianna screamed. I ran to the door. The King and Queen of Hearts struggled inside the room. Cory and Arianna.

"Let her go!" I shouted.

"What are you doing here?" Cory shoved Arianna on the bed, grabbed me and slammed the door. I struggled against him, but he was stronger than I was.

"Run," I yelled to Arianna. "Get help."

She dashed for the door, but he grabbed her with his free arm. Now he had both of us. Arianna began to sob.

"Fight him," I told her. "Don't give up."

He yanked me tighter under his arm, and I felt as if I were being cut in half.

"You aren't getting away, so just calm down, both of you," he said. "Don't make me hurt you."

"You did this because you think she destroyed your life," I told him. "Because she wanted to be a star on her own. You don't really love her, either. You're just pissed because you know you have more talent than Josh and Arianna put together."

"You're right about that. After what she put me through, I deserve every dime I'll get from this."

"The police will be here any minute," I said. "If you ever want to take back your musical career, you had better get out right now."

"Everyone will assume that we left the building. They won't think to look here."

"Yes, they will. Stacy's going to tell Henry Jaffa."

"Stacy?" He laughed. "She isn't going to tell anyone anything."

"Of course she is," I said. "She has nothing to lose now."

"I'm not so sure about that." He grinned. The door behind us opened. Stacy walked inside without her mask, still wearing Arianna's Madonna costume.

"I see you found them." She gave me a smile that was so scary I had to look away.

"Stacy," Arianna gasped. "You bitch."

"Watch your mouth. All you mean to me now is ransom money."

"But it was your idea for us to do this."

"It was a good idea, too. The best idea I could come up with." She walked up to us and took a proprietary stand beside Cory. "Until he came along."

It was the worst example of Gemini backstabbing I had ever witnessed. She had planned with Arianna to fake her own kidnapping, and instead, had decided to partner with Cory and kidnap Arianna for real. It could work, too. They would get enough from Arianna's family to disappear for good. I needed to get in touch with Jaffa. I stopped struggling against Cory, inched my hand into my pocket, and pressed Jaffa's number into my phone. Thank goodness, Cory didn't have Ms. Bodmer's built-in cell detector.

"That's better," he said, and let go of Arianna and me. "Don't even think about running for the door."

"You cut the phone line in the hotel elevator," I said. "Didn't you, Stacy?"

"I was making sure we could hold it at the eleventh floor. Trying to figure out how long it would take to get in and out." She looked up at Cory. "We need to get moving, hon."

"What happens when she gets tired of you?" I asked, speaking up for the sake of the phone.

"We'll have so much money that it won't matter."

"What about your career?"

"That's over, thanks to Arianna. You two are such good friends that you can have a nice little evening in front of the television. I'm sorry, but I'm going to have to tie you up now."

"Don't do it," I said. "You're a Scorpio, Cory. You know what that means about dwelling in the past. You've got to get unstuck and focus on your career. You know this whole kidnapping thing was Stacy's idea. You can still back out."

"Why would he want to?" she snapped. "If his career were going anywhere, it already would have happened."

"Not when he's trapped by his resentment and emotions."

"Spare me the astrology," she said. "Come on, Cory. We need to finish this and get out of here."

I yanked my phone out of my pocket and shouted, "Mr. Jaffa, hurry. We're on the eleventh floor. Stacy is down here with Arianna and me. She's the one behind Arianna's kidnapping. She . . ."

Stacy knocked the phone out of my hand to the floor. "What the hell are you doing?" she demanded.

"Calling Jaffa." I turned to Cory. "You can still have the career. Telling the truth about Stacy could get you the right kind of publicity. Don't give up everything for her because, believe me, she won't give up anything for you."

"Anybody here?" a male voice called from down the hall.

"Help us!" Arianna screamed.

Cory shoved her toward me and ran out the door. Her body hit me hard, and we both fell. I was still trying to help her to her feet when the others found us.

"They're lying," Stacy shouted, and took off in the direction Cory had gone.

I knew she would not get far.

Henry Jaffa appeared in the doorway. He stepped inside and reached out his arm to steady me. I leaned against the velvet bird on his shoulder and felt tears in my eyes.

"I'm so sorry," he said, and the kindness in his voice broke my heart.

⁓

I cried that night, sitting on the edge of the bed in that room where Arianna and I would have been held captive. For the first time since Jeremy left, and my parents had sat me down for the divorce talk, I just let go and bawled out every sorrow. Arianna cried too.

The police had left, and we were waiting for her mother to arrive to take her home. Someone had given her a jacket that she had put on over the Queen of Hearts costume. She looked like a little kid playing dress-up.

"I'm so ashamed," she said. Tears streaked her face. "How did I get so low that I would even consider doing something as crazy as that?"

"Stacy can be pretty persuasive," I said and wiped my eyes. "She's the bad Twin. You're the good one."

"No, I'm not. I am such a loser. Josh was disgusted. I know I've lost him this time."

"I don't think so. He loves you." That brought on a new round of tears from both of us.

"I'm sorry I was so horrible to you, Logan," she said. "I thought if I introduced you to Cory, you'd get distracted from the astro thing and trying to investigate Alex Keen. I knew you suspected something was going to happen tonight."

"What about Alex Keen?" I stopped before I revealed what I knew about that situation.

She shook her head sadly. "That's really what broke Josh and me up the last time. When I did the Canadian tour last year, Alex decided he was crazy about me for a hot second. I called him the night you came to San Francisco, and he came by after you left so that we could get our stories straight."

"Why would you want to lie?" I asked.

"Publicity. Dating me wouldn't be good for his image. But the boy has his secrets. Don't let those eyes fool you."

"You have to tell me," I said. "For my friend's sake. She thinks he's into her now."

"He won't be for long. Besides, he's a kid." She got up from the bed and turned to face me with a smile that was still more sadness than anything else. "Alex Keen pretends to be this sexy young chef. He just doesn't say how young. He's only seventeen."

Alex Keen, celebrity chef and wannabe womanizer, was a teen. What a weird ending to this outrageous day. No wonder he made sure his birth year didn't show up anywhere. It wasn't the fact that he was so young that bothered me. It was his deception. Enough people had been hurt tonight. I didn't want Chili to have to join that club.

24

EACH SIGN HAS ITS OWN CHALLENGE TO OVERCOME. AN ARIES LEARNS TO CHOOSE BATTLES. A TAURUS LEARNS THAT SOMETIMES WE MUST LET GO. A LEO LEARNS IT'S OKAY TO SHARE THE STAGE. A GEMINI LEARNS THAT WORDS ARE NOT ALWAYS ENOUGH. A CANCER LEARNS THAT NO ONE LIKES VICTIMS. A VIRGO LEARNS THAT PERFECT PLANNING DOES NOT GUARANTEE SUCCESS. A LIBRA LEARNS TO TAKE A STAND. A SCORPIO LEARNS TO SPEAK UP. A SAGITTARIUS LEARNS TO LISTEN. A CAPRICORN LEARNS TO LIGHTEN UP. AN AQUARIUS LEARNS THAT BRILLIANT IDEAS MUST BE PUT INTO ACTION. A PISCES LEARNS THAT ALL OF THE DREAMING IN THE WORLD WILL NOT

MAKE IT SO. A WISE PERSON LEARNS. EVERYONE ELSE
KEEPS MAKING THE SAME MISTAKES.

—Fearless Astrology

rianna and I walked back up to the suite together.
Almost everyone had gone. Paige spoke quietly with
Graciela Perez. Chili and Alex sat at a table with
Bobby, Mary Elizabeth, and a couple of other people from the
magazine. I still wasn't sure how I was going to tell Chili that
her sophisticated celebrity chef was a teenager.

Everyone turned to look at us as we came inside.

"I need to just hide out and get my life together," Arianna
whispered, "but I don't know where to go."

I thought of Terra Bella Beach, where everything was low-
key and laid back. Where some people still left their houses
unlocked at night.

"Let's talk later," I said. "Maybe we can come up with
something."

Just then Josh stepped out from the catering suite. He had
changed out of his Dr. Jekyll costume and had on jeans and
a deep brown sweater the color of his hair.

He flashed that bleach-strip smile and put out his arms.

Arianna whimpered and ran to him. I stood watching. At
least something had turned out right.

y Sherlock notebook had come in handy after all. Josh and Arianna left with her mom. I sat trying to look invisible and gazed out at the city while Chili and Paige said their goodbyes to Alex and Graciela. I had made enough notes about the evening's events to almost fill it when I became aware of someone behind me.

"What a night." Henry Jaffa sat down beside me. He had ditched the coat and raven. Only the forgotten moustache remained. "I had no idea about Stacy," he said. "I just thought she was, well, ambitious."

"She wanted the glory, that's for sure, and she didn't care how she got it."

"If you hadn't become involved, she might have pulled it off. You realize that, don't you?"

I hadn't thought about it. Could he be right? "And all I wanted was the astrology column. Funny how important it seemed, at the time." I bit my lip to keep from crying again.

"I hope you'll forgive a personal question," he said, "but is there something going on in your life right now?"

"The usual stuff," I told him. "Parents getting divorced, boyfriend not into me."

"You know, there's a theory—I'm not sure how accurate it is—that bad experiences actually make one a better writer."

"I remember reading something about that in one of your interviews," I said. "I sure hope it's true. Thank you for all you've tried to do for me, Mr. Jaffa. I can't tell you how much it means to me."

He gave me that weird but warm Aquarius grin. "Don't you think it's time you called me Henry? All of my writers do."

My lip trembled. Couldn't help it. Thank goodness I was an Aquarius like him. I managed a weird grin of my own.

"Yes, Henry," I said. "I guess it is."

NOTES TO SELF

Now I'm one of the people—one of the writers—who get to call Henry Jaffa just Henry. Stacy had been one of those people once. Now, her worst fears would be realized, and she would lose her job and probably a great deal more. Still, the Gemini had managed to fool Henry Jaffa. She might even be able to talk herself out of this situation.

The next day as we got ready to drive home, I opened the front car door and stepped aside.

"About time," Paige said, and climbed inside. "From now on, we can take turns."

CRUSHES: HOW TO FASCINATE A PISCES
By Logan McRae

This dreamy Water sign lives in his head. He's the guy staring out the window in class, unaware that the teacher has just called on him. Even the most intelligent Pisces can stumble trying to get out the right words when he's nervous. And he usually is nervous when attention is focused on him.

Kind, caring, and sympathetic, he often lacks assertiveness, at least until you get to know him better and discover that wicked Pisces sense of humor. Because of his gentle nature, many mistake him for a doormat and try to take advantage of him. Bad idea. Misjudging or trying to manipulate this guy will keep you from ever getting close to him.

He loves anything creative—art, music, writing—and is attracted to girls who share these interests. However, you could be the most creative creature on the planet, but if you use that creativity to put people down or make jokes at the expense of others, the Fish will swim right on past you.
In his fantasy life, there's a perfect girl for him out there, one who will understand him and share his dreams and goals.

Here are three ways to be that girl:

• **Be yourself.** *Pisces doesn't judge. He can spot a phony the moment she opens her mouth, and sometimes sooner. This is one guy who will accept and value your vulnerable side.*

• **Share your dreams.** *The bigger the better. This guy won't tell you that you're crazy or that you should be more practical. His dreams are as big as yours.*

• **Be calm.** *This guy is searching for inner peace, and a tranquil, even mystical vibe will appeal to him. Talk about meditating and yoga. Carry intriguing books on spirituality, mythology, magic, astrology, and be ready to discuss them when he notices. Because he will.*

What to say when he asks you out: *"I've been dreaming that you would call me."*

YOUR SUN SIGN ISN'T A LIFE SENTENCE. IT IS A MENU OF POSSIBILITIES. ARIES CAN SETTLE DOWN. TAURUS CAN BE FLEXIBLE. GEMINI CAN BE FAITHFUL. CANCER CAN CONQUER THOSE MOODS. LEO CAN SHARE THE STAGE. VIRGO CAN RELAX AND SEE WHAT'S RIGHT AS WELL AS WHAT ISN'T. LIBRA CAN COMMIT. SCORPIO CAN FORGIVE. SAGITTARIUS CAN LEARN TO LISTEN. CAPRICORN CAN LIGHTEN UP. AQUARIUS CAN ACT IMPULSIVELY. AND PISCES CAN TAKE THE SPOTLIGHT. THAT'S WHAT BEING AN EVOLVED SIGN IS ALL ABOUT. YOU CAN BE WHATEVER YOU WANT TO BE.

—Fearless Astrology

*T*he party was almost two weeks ago. It's already November, and the changes have been as crazy as the weather. I have been cold all day, but it doesn't have much to do with the sharp wind. I've felt this way since I talked to Jeremy's girlfriend, and I can no longer ignore the fact that my summer with him is far behind me.

My dad agreed to let my new friend from Los Angeles come to stay in our guestroom for a couple of weeks. I didn't mention that the Gemini friend would be arriving with a few secrets and a lot of baggage. For now, at least, it looks as if that was a wise decision. Arianna stayed with us until the media heat died down. Tonight she will return to L.A. with Josh.

Alex Keen thanked Chili for her mom's Armenian recipes and said they had "influenced" him for some of the material in his new cookbook. He'll list her in the acknowledgments, of course. And, by the way, he has a girlfriend in Napa. Underage or not, that unevolved Sadge has lived up to the most unreliable aspects of his sign.

The official story is that Stacy resigned from her position. Mary Elizabeth is the new editor of *CRUSH*. When that was announced, Danielle, Stacy's assistant, quit on the spot. Mary Elizabeth told me that although I still have my internship, she has decided against an astrology column. At least for now. As my Gram Janie says, you win some, you lose some, and you refuse some.

So, yes, I wrote all of the *CRUSH* love columns for nothing. But maybe not. I learned a lot about how different Sun signs fall for each other. Maybe that information will come in handy one day.

Jeremy tried to phone me twice. Both times the message on my voicemail was too garbled to hear. All I got was, "traveling in Ireland with my dad" and "a girl I met." One day we will speak, and I will force myself to wish him well and pretend that I am not devastated by the way he left me.

Terra High will still be featured in the beach issue of *CRUSH*. Today the rain has stopped, and we'll actually be able to see the sun setting at our photo shoot this evening. Odd that an evening beach shoot will have to take place beneath coming-and-going storm clouds, but that's the way it is here on the California coast. Sweaters in summer. Bikinis in the rain. The uncertainty is part of what I love about this place.

I'm riding in front again, and I have to admit, I like it better up here. But it's worth the backseat to see the way Paige has come out of her shell. I never realized how we just assumed it was her job to take up the rear. Being a Pisces, she had assumed it too. No more, though.

She's in taupe, and Chili in a short strapless black-and-white print, belted at the waist. My white pants are rolled up, and the shirt over my white tank is that orange sherbet color kids in the rest of the country think California girls wear every day.

There's a knot in my stomach, a twinge of anticipation. It's as if I've had back-to-back espressos since morning, and I realize that for the first time since the party, I am actually excited about something.

As we pull into the school parking lot this late Saturday afternoon, I see that Sol is already there. He has dressed California style as well, in shorts and a pale blue shirt that accentuates his eyes. I remember that he's been wearing that color all week.

I get out of the car and say, "Hey, Sol."

"How's it goin'?" he replies in a bored kind of way. He's acted like that all week too.

"What's the matter?" I ask.

"Nothing. I'm just waiting for my girlfriend."

"Your girlfriend?" Cute as he is, he's not for me.

"You sound surprised." He gives me a wounded Cancer smile that he probably thinks is soulful.

"Not at all," I say. "Good for you."

"And you're still into that Ireland guy?"

"Yes, I am," I say, and pretend to look happy.

Just then Kat's car screeches up beside us.

"Freaking watch it," Chili shouts. "You almost ran over us."

"Sorry. That would be a shame." She gets out wearing her cheer outfit, of course, and flounces up to Sol.

What follows is a PDA of such proportion that it would get both of them sent straight to the Student Responsibility Center if a civic-minded teacher were watching. Then, Kat takes Sol's hand, shoots us a smug, self-satisfied look, and heads for the campus.

"Terra High, Terra High," Chili chants as they walk away.

"Poor guy," I say. "She'll burn through him in a week."

"He deserves better." Chili eyes me as if to say that I should have taken advantage of her efforts to get Sol and me together.

The magazine people are already here. I realize that I should have brought a sweater. Bobby waves from the other side of the grassy area that leads to the beach. They will snap some photos here, and then, we'll walk down to the water, where they will take the celeb shots.

There he is, the official Terra High celeb, Josh Mellick, his deep brown hair spiked, wearing shorts and a shirt that makes his teeth gleam even whiter. Alex Keen was supposed to have had the job but was replaced at the last minute. The gossip leak about his age and his true-to-his-Sadge sign love life might be getting him lots of publicity, but not in *CRUSH*.

Josh drove in from L.A. earlier today, and we all had lunch at Chili's house. As thrilled as Chili's mom Stella was, she respected Arianna's desire for privacy and restrained herself from inviting the entire neighborhood to drop by. Arianna is still there, probably getting cooking lessons and a month's supply of food. I'll miss her when she goes back, but I'm pretty sure her life is finally on track now.

Josh joins the photographer and Bobby, and grins at us.

"I'm impressed." Bodmer walks up to me. She's secured her thick curls with a long scarf, but already many have escaped. Her glasses are poked into her hair, as usual, like a leopard-print headband. "You actually know Josh Mellick. How cool is that?"

"Hi, Ms. Bodmer," I say. "I'm glad you came."

"It's too good to miss, even on a Saturday. I'm here to cheer you on, girls."

"Hey," Bobby yells to the photographer. "Get the teach in one of the shots."

Bodmer squeals and heads toward him.

It's time now.

I turn to look at Paige. She's perfect with her pale hair floating behind her and her white eyelet shirt covering a taupe mesh Graciela Perez swimsuit. It's called a monokini, but it's mega everything. Paige is even more killer than she was in the Aphrodite costume.

"Ready?" I ask her.

She gives me a shy smile. "I still can't believe this. It should have been you or Chili."

"Stop it," I say. "If anyone is California beach, you are, Paige. Graciela was right about that."

"Besides . . . ," Chili grins. ". . . I told you guys from the start that I didn't really want it. I just didn't want Kat to get it."

We pose for more group shots and then walk to the beach, where Paige smiles up at Josh in the sand, hands behind her back. White tide swirl around their bare ankles. I can already see how they will look in the magazine, his tanned good looks a backdrop for her understated beauty.

The sun starts to set in the brilliant purples and pinks. They slip into the ocean, which now looks like shimmering black glass. Standing beside Chili, I realize that my skin is so icy my teeth are almost chattering. I need to borrow someone's jacket or just head home.

Except that something is wrong. Chili is staring at me in a strange way, her eyes wide.

"Logan." Her voice is part-whisper, part-gasp. "Look!"

I turn in the direction she has pointed. A form is coming toward me, walking fast, no, not walking, running now. That's all he is for the first moment, just a figure heading toward me in the sand. Not one of the kids from school, though. He's dressed in jeans and a khaki jacket. *That* khaki jacket. In the wind, his dark hair whips around his face. A face I would know anywhere.

Jeremy. After all he has done to me, why is he here? I stumble through the sand, tears and wind burning my eyes.

"Jeremy," I call out, unable to believe what I am seeing.

"I had to find you, Logan. I tried to call you, left messages. Didn't you get them?"

"Only a word or two came through." I grab his face in my hands and stare into those fierce eyes. "What happened? Who is Tori?"

"The daughter of my dad's girlfriend who's been visiting from Boston. She decided she was in love with me, but nothing happened with us, I swear. She's nuts, a stalker chick. She even stole my phone."

"I know. She answered when I called. I thought . . ."

"And I couldn't figure out why I didn't hear from you. And then, by the time I realized what was going on, I was on tour with my dad. So . . ." He gives me that possessive Taurus smile. ". . . I just got on a plane."

"How'd you know where to find me?"

"Your dad. He's a nice guy."

"And you flew all the way from Dublin?"

"Yeah. To tell you I love you." Now he's pressing his hands against my face. "I love you, Logan."

I throw my arms around him and feel his arms wrap around me. We hug the breath from each other, and I inhale the sweet smell of his hair.

I'm vaguely aware of the others. Sol and Kat, who walk by, arms around each other. Chili. Then Paige, chatting with Bobby and the photographer. Other kids, Bodmer, the magazine crew.

And, yes, it's technically a PDA in front of the entire school, but I don't care. Right now I have everything I thought I had lost. And I've gotten back something else too, something I can only begin to understand right now.

"I love you, too," I say. "I never stopped."

He kisses me again, then steps back and slowly runs his hands along my bare arms. "You're shivering," he says. "Let's go somewhere quiet. Get some coffee. Talk."

"Sounds good." I place my hands over his, and no longer feel the cold.

We wrap our arms around each other and walk down the beach toward the street, matching our footsteps in perfect rhythm. The crashing waves sound surreal, as if it is summer again, and we are back in Monterey. But, no. Jeremy is here, in Terra Bella Beach. He has come all this way to find me.

"What about you?" His voice is harsh against my cheek. "You haven't met anyone else, have you?"

"Of course not. You're all I could think about. I was so confused."

"And you haven't been getting in trouble with that astrology stuff again, have you?"

I look up into those teasing, soulful Taurus eyes. "Now, that," I tell him, "is a story too long and complicated to go into just yet."

Too long and complicated, yes. Too insignificant. And too far away, right now, from my Aquarius mind, to even matter.

WHAT'S YOUR SUN SIGN?

SIX TRAITS EACH. REMEMBER, THE SUN IS NOT THE SUM. IT IS ONLY THE BEGINNING.

—*Fearless Astrology*

Aries: **March 21–22 to April 19–20**

Energetic, Enthusiastic, Take-charge, Self-centered,
Quick-tempered, Aggressive
You value: *Attention*

Taurus: **April 20–21 to May 20–21**

Reliable, Kind-hearted, Sensuous,
Stubborn, Judgmental, Lazy
You value: *Stability*

Gemini: **May 21–22 to June 21–22**

Strong communicator, Versatile, Generous,
Fickle, Scattered, Nervous
You value: *Intellect*

Cancer: **June 22–23 to July 22–23**

Nurturing, Traditional, Family-oriented,
Codependent, Clingy, Moody
You value: *Empathy*

Leo: **July 23–24 to Aug 23–24**

Leader, Full of fun, Warm and
loving, Overbearing, Attention-seeking, Insensitive
You value: *Creativity*

Virgo: **Aug 23–24 to Sept 23–24**

Nitpicky, Helpful, Methodical, Shy, Critical, Cheap
You value: *Organization*

Libra: **Sept 23–24 to Oct 23–24**

Attracted to beauty, Charming, Flexible,
Wishy-washy, Manipulative, Jealous
You value: *Fairness*

Scorpio: **Oct 24–25 to Nov 21–22**

Intense, Passionate, Secretive, Compulsive,
Sarcastic, Vindictive
You value: *Loyalty*

Sagittarius: **Nov 22–23 to Dec 21–22**

Optimistic, Goal-oriented, Independent,
A loner, Restless, Blunt
You value: *Adventure*

Capricorn: **Dec 22–23 to Jan 19–20**

Hard-working, Disciplined, Trustworthy,
Rigid, Dominating, Overly disciplined
You value: *Determination*

Aquarius: **Jan 20–21 to Feb 18–19**

Friendly, Caring, Humanitarian, Nonconformist,
Eccentric, Just plain weird
You value: *Humanity*

Pisces: **Feb 19–20 to March 20–21**

Sensitive, Compassionate, Creative,
Self-sacrificing, Dreamy, Introverted
You value: *Imagination*

Bonnie Hearn Hill is a Gemini, a full-time writer and a former editor for a daily newspaper. She is the author of INTERN and five other adult thriller novels, and teaches writing in her hometown of Fresno, California and on Writer's Digest Online. She also mentors writers and speaks at numerous writing conferences. Read more about Bonnie and your astrological sign at: www.bonniehearnhill.com